TENANT FOR
DEATH

TENANT FOR DEATH

CYRIL HARE

HarperPerennial

A Division of HarperCollins*Publishers*

This work was originally published in England by Faber & Faber, Ltd. in 1937. It is here reprinted by arrangement.

First Perennial Library edition published 1982. First HarperPerennial edition published 1991.

ISBN 0-06-080570-6

91 92 93 94 95 WB/OPM 10 9 8 7 6 5 4 3 2 1

To
M.B.G.C.

TENANT FOR
DEATH

1

Jackie Roach

Daylesford Gardens, S.W., is one of those addresses
that make the most experienced of taxi-drivers hesitate for a moment or two when you give it. Not that
he will have any difficulty in determining its general
direction, which is in that quiet and respectable region
where South Kensington borders on Chelsea. The trouble arises from the lack of imagination displayed by the
building syndicate which first laid out the Daylesford
estate some time in the middle of the last century. For
besides Daylesford Gardens, there are Daylesford Terrace, Daylesford Square, Upper and Lower Daylesford
Streets, not to mention a tall, raw red-brick block of
flats known as Daylesford Court Mansions and two or
three new and almost smart little houses which still keep
the name of Daylesford Mews. The houses in Daylesford
Gardens, however, are neither raw, tall, nor red-brick,
nor new, nor anything approaching smart. On the contrary, they are squat, yellow and elderly, bearing on their
monotonous three-storied fronts the same dingy livery of
stucco, drab but—with an effort—respectable. One or two

1

have sunk so far as to become boarding-houses, several may be suspected of paying guests, but for the most part they still contrive to carry on the unequal warfare against adverse circumstances and keep the banner of gentility flying.

House agents have been known to call the district a "retired" one, and the description is just in more ways than one. It certainly suits almost all the inhabitants of the Gardens. They are pre-eminently the refuge of the not too wealthy middle-aged. Retired colonels and County Court judges, ex-Civil Servants and half-pay naval officers, with one or two lean sallow-faced men who have in their time perhaps governed districts half as large as England, now share between them the empire of the muddy grass and draggled laurustinus bushes which constitute "the gardens". Their houses, too, discreet and unassuming, seem also to have retired from whatever busy existence they may once have had, and to be awaiting with dignified resignation the fate that is in store for London houses when the building lease falls in.

At the northern end of Daylesford Gardens, where Upper Daylesford Street, noisy with omnibuses and motor vans, marks the boundary of the old Daylesford property, Jackie Roach, the newspaper seller, had his pitch. Every evening he was to be seen there, his comic blob of a nose wobbling uncertainly above his ragged red moustache in time to his husky chant of *"News—Star—Standard!"* Most of the householders in the Gardens knew him by sight. How much he knew about them, their circumstances, habits and domestic staffs, few of them—probably ever guessed. They were, as he put it, among his "regulars", and it was almost a point of honour with him to be acquainted with their affairs. He knew—and liked—old Colonel Petherington at No. 15, with his threadbare grey suit and erect habit of body, who went

2

so punctually to his club every afternoon and returned so punctually every evening for dinner. He knew—and disliked—the flashy Mrs. Brent at No. 34, and could have told her husband something of the man who came to visit her when he was away, if he had ever thought of enquiring in that direction. He knew the quiet, shy Miss Penrose of No. 27, whose maid, Rosa, came so regularly at six o'clock every evening for the *Standard*, and could always be relied upon for a few minutes' gossip.

On this chill, windy evening, Roach would have been glad of a little chat with anyone who would stop to pass the time of day—anything to keep his mind off the rheumatism that always tortured him at this time of year. But nobody felt like stopping now. They only paused long enough to thrust a copper into Jackie's hand and snatch a paper, for all the world as though a chap was an automatic machine. Rosa was different. Whatever the weather, she would always hang about a bit for a chat at the corner, as well she might indeed, with a warm back kitchen to go home to.

But no Rosa would come this evening. For a month past Miss Penrose had been away. She had gone abroad, and Rosa had gone to her family in the country. The house was let furnished to a Mr. Colin James. Roach knew his name, thanks to a nodding acquaintance with Crabtree, the manservant who had usurped Rosa's place at No. 27, but he had never spoken to him, or even sold him newspapers. Unlike most of the other inhabitants of the Gardens, he was still in business. At least, nearly every morning he took an eastward bound bus from the corner, and came back again in the evening, so his business was to be presumed. Roach did not like him the better for it. He felt obscurely that such behaviour was letting the Gardens down.

3

At about half-past six, when the throng in Upper Daylesford Street was at its height and the long-threatening rain had begun to spatter down, Roach, fumbling with numbed fingers for elevenpence change, caught sight of Mr. James on the other side of the street. There was, as he afterwards explained to certain interested persons, no mistaking Mr. James. For one thing, he was the only resident in Daylesford Gardens with a beard. It was no mere apologetic tuft, either, but a bushy mass of brown hair, that fairly covered his face from the mouth down. Then there was his figure. He was noticeably fat, with a fatness that seemed quite out of proportion to his thin legs, so that he walked always with a cautious waddle, as though afraid that his weight would overbalance him. Roach noted the passing of the familiar ungainly shape without interest. Then something made him look round again, and stare after him with renewed attention. That something was the simple fact that on this occasion, Mr. James was accompanied by another person.

"The old—what lives by 'isself," was Roach's private description of Mr. James. Most of the Gardens' inhabitants, indeed, were of the type that keep themselves to themselves. Roach respected them all the more for that. But Mr. James was of them all the most completely alone. During his short residence at No. 27, no visitor had ever been known to cross the threshold, not so much as a letter or parcel, so Crabtree asserted, had ever been delivered there. And never, until now, had he seen Mr. Colin James in the street except alone.

But this time—there could be no doubt of it—Mr. James had found a friend. Or if not a friend, at any rate a near acquaintance, to judge from the way they went along the pavement side by side, their heads close together, as though in quiet, earnest discussion. A pity, thought Roach, that the stranger was on the far side as they went round the corner, so that James's great bulk blotted him out completely. Just for curiosity's sake, he would like to have known—"News, sir? Yessir! Fi'pence change, thank you, sir!"

He screwed his head round to look down the Gardens. There was a lamp-post opposite No. 27, and the couple were just within its beams. The light shone on the yellow-brown bag which Mr. James always carried. They stopped and Mr. James was evidently fumbling for his key. Then he opened the door, went in and the stranger followed him. Roach, as he turned to thrust a paper into the hand of a customer, felt oddly triumphant. Mr. James had a visitor! In a small way, it was as though a long-standing record had been broken.

Nearly an hour later, the newspaper seller finally left his pitch. The rain was now a steady downpour. The street was wet and deserted. The "Crown" in Lower Daylesford Street would by contrast be warm and friendly. Cold and thirsty, Roach sheltered his papers beneath his arm and set off in the direction which James had taken before him, but upon the other side of the street. He was halfway down it, his eyes fixed on the pavement, his thoughts on the refreshment that awaited him, when the sound of a street door closing made him look up. He was opposite No. 27, and a familiar figure, carrying the inevitable bag, had just emerged, and was now walking away towards the upper end of the Gardens.

"Old Man-of-Mystery again!" said Roach to himself. "What's he done to his pal, I wonder?"

He reflected, as he went on his way, that he had never before seen Mr. James walk so fast. Two minutes later he was standing in an infinitely pleasant, muggy atmosphere before a crowded bar.

" 'Ow's trade, Jacko?" asked an acquaintance.

"Rotten bloody awful," answered Jackie, a tankard to his lips. "There ain't nothing in the papers nowadays 'cept this political stuff. What we want to make 'em sell is a murder." He took a long pull and repeated, smacking his lips: "Murder—bloody murder, that's the ticket!"

2

The Twelve Apostles

Saturday, November 14th

The London and Imperial Estates Company, Ltd., and its eleven associated companies, familiarly known on the Stock Exchange as "The Twelve Apostles", occupied imposing offices in Lothbury. There were eight storeys in all, a grandiose Portland stone façade without, waxed oak panels within. The entrance hall was adorned with pillars of polished marble, and was guarded by the largest and smartest commissionaire in the City of London. On the floors above, large airy rooms housed during business hours regiments of typists, clerks, and office boys. In smaller and more luxurious apartments, their superiors—managers, accountants and heads of departments—pursued their mysterious and, presumably, profitable ways. But to the man in the street, and more particularly to the investor or speculator in the City, all this splendour was summed up in and made significant by the personality of one man—Lionel Ballantine.

Ballantine was one of those picturesque figures appearing from time to time in the financial world of London, whose activities lend colour to the ordinarily drab record of commerce. He was, in the generally accepted sense of the phrase, one of the best known men in the City. That is to say, a large public was familiar through the papers with his outward appearance and that of his country house, his racing stables, his yacht and his herd of pedigree Jerseys. A smaller and more closely interested public knew something, though not as much as it would have wished, of his financial interests. In actual fact, the man himself was probably as little known as it is possible to be. He had no intimate friends and even his closest associates knew how far they were from possessing his full confidence. His origin was obscure, and if many people would have liked to penetrate the veil in which he chose to shroud it, there were more who contented themselves with prophesying, cynically or blasphemously, as to his future.

By the world in general, however, Ballantine was taken as what he appeared to be—a spectacularly successful business man. In a comparatively short space of time, he had risen from nothing—or at least from very little—to a position of genuine importance and even power. Such a career is never to be achieved save at the cost of a good deal of jealousy and detraction, and he had received his fair share of both. More than once there had been unpleasant whispers as to his methods, and on one occasion—the famous Fanshawe Bank failure of four years before—something louder than whispers. But each time the murmurs had died down, leaving Ballantine more prosperous than ever.

But now the whispers were beginning to be heard again in many places, and nowhere more urgently than in the little ante-room to Ballantine's private office on the top floor of the great building. Here the affairs of the company were being discussed in low tones by two of its employees.

"I tell you, Johnson," said one, "I don't like the look of things. Here's the Annual General Meeting not two weeks away, and the market's getting jumpy. Have you seen this morning's figures?"

"The market!" said the other contemptuously. "The market's always got nerves. We've been through worse scares than this, haven't we? Remember what happened in '29? Well, then—"

"I'll tell you another thing," went on the first speaker without listening to the interruption. "Du Pine has got the jumps too. Have you seen him this morning? He was absolutely green. I tell you, he knows something."

"Where is he now?" asked Johnson. "In there?" He nodded his head to a glass-panelled door labelled "Secretary".

"No. He's in the old man's room. Been in and out there the last half-hour, like a cat with the fidgets. And the old man isn't there either."

"Well, what of it? Would he be, on a Saturday morning?"

"Yes, he would—this morning. He's got an appointment for eleven o'clock. I was here when Du Pine made it for him."

"An appointment? Who with?"

"Robinson, the Southern Bank man. And he's bringing Prufrock with him."

"Prufrock? The solicitor?"

"That's him."

Johnson whistled softly. Then he said after a noticeable pause:

"Percy, old man, I suppose you don't happen to know what it was they were coming to see him about, do you?"

"What are you getting at?"

"I mean, if it was the Redbury bond issue they were asking about, and if old Prufrock starts nosing round—"

"Well?" said Percy. "Suppose it was. You had the handling of that issue, hadn't you? What about it?"

Johnson was looking straight in front of him. He looked right through the wall and saw a trim red-brick villa at Ealing, heavily mortgaged and utterly desirable, with two small children playing on its minute scrap of lawn, and his wife on the doorstep watching them.

"Well?" Percy repeated.

Johnson turned his head.

"I was just thinking," he said. "A pal of mine in Garrisons' told me there was a head clerk's job going there. It would mean dropping fifty a year, but—I think I shall put in for it, Percy old man."

An understanding glance passed between the two men, but before either could speak the telephone on the table between them rang. At the same moment the door of Ballantine's private room opened and Du Pine, the secretary to the company, walked quickly out. He picked up the receiver, barked into it: "Send them up at once!" and had disappeared again in the space of a few seconds.

"You see what I mean?" murmured Percy. "Nervy, eh?"

"I suppose that was Robinson and Prufrock," said Johnson, rising to his feet. "Well, I'm going round to Garrisons', *now*."

In the inner room, Du Pine took a deep breath and squared his thin shoulders, like a man preparing to face an assault. For a moment he stood thus, then relaxed. His hands, which he had kept still during that brief space by an effort of will, began to jump uneasily from the wrists. He paced the room twice in each direction, then came to a halt opposite a looking-glass. He saw in it a face which would have been handsome but for the unhealthy sallowness of the cheeks, black hair neatly brushed down, a pair of bright beady eyes with heavy lines beneath them.

10

He was still staring at the reflection, as though at the portrait of a stranger, when the visitors were announced.

Du Pine spun round on his heel.

"Good morning, gentlemen!" he exclaimed.

"You are Mr. Du Pine, I think?" said the solicitor.

"At your service, Mr. Prufrock, I think? Mr. Robinson I have met before. Won't you sit down?"

Mr. Prufrock did not sit down, still standing, he looked slowly round the room.

"Our appointment was with Mr. Ballantine," he said.

"Quite so," answered Du Pine easily. "Quite so. But he is unfortunately not able to be here in person this morning, and has asked me to deal with the matter in his absence."

Mr. Prufrock's eyebrows went up in shocked surprise. Mr. Robinson's, on the other hand, came down in a threatening frown. It would be difficult to say which of the two expressions Du Pine found the more unpleasant.

"Mr. Ballantine has asked you—*you*—to deal with this matter in his absence?" repeated the solicitor incredulously. "With the Redbury bond issue? May I remind you once more that we have a personal appointment with Mr. Ballantine?"

"Just so," said Du Pine, beginning to show signs of nervousness. "Just so. And I can assure you, gentlemen, that Mr. Ballantine would certainly be here if—if he could."

"What do you mean? Is he unwell?"

Du Pine indicated assent.

"That seems very strange. He seemed in perfect health yesterday. Can you tell me what form his illness takes?"

"No, I cannot."

"Very well. Then we can assume that it is not serious. I think that the best thing would be for us to make an appointment to see him at his private house."

11

Robinson here spoke for the first time.

"I rather doubt whether we should find him there, well or ill," he observed. "If I might make the suggestion, it would be more to the purpose to enquire for him at the house of Mrs. Eales—his mistress," he added in an aside to Prufrock, who pursed his lips and sniffed by way of reply.

"I have done so already," Du Pine broke in. "He is not there."

"I see." The solicitor looked very steadily at him for a moment, to give his next question its full weight. "Mr. Du Pine, will you please answer me directly: Do you know where Mr. Ballantine is?"

Du Pine took a deep breath, like a swimmer before the plunge, and then began to speak at a great pace.

"No, I do not. And I am quite aware that in the circumstances Mr. Ballantine's absence may seem rather—that it is a matter which calls for enquiry. But—gentlemen—before you put any construction on it—before you take any steps which—any irrevocable steps—there is one matter that—in fairness to Mr. Ballantine—in fairness to myself—it may be of importance in the future—"

"Well?"

"Mr. Ballantine had a visitor here yesterday morning, who disturbed him very much. It may in some way account for anything erratic in his behavior—"

Prufrock turned to Robinson. His mouth was set in a hard line.

"Really, Robinson, I think we are wasting our time here," he said.

"But, gentlemen, this is important," Du Pine insisted.

"I can hardly think of any visitor yesterday who was more important to Mr. Ballantine than the appointment he had made for today," said Prufrock drily.

"But I can assure you, sir, I can assure you that Mr. Ballantine had every intention of meeting you today. He had a perfect explanation of any little discrepancies there might be in the bond issue. There is only one possible explanation for his not coming, and that is that he was not physically able to come."

"What is all this nonsense?" Robinson spoke wearily. "And what has this mysterious visitor to do with it?"

"Perhaps you will understand when I tell you that the visitor was Mr. Fanshawe—"

The two men stiffened with interest.

"Fanshawe?" echoed Prufrock. "He's still in gaol, isn't he?"

"His sentence is about due to expire," put in Robinson. "Poor fellow, I knew him well before. . . ."

"—And that he threatened him, in my hearing," went on Du Pine wildly. "Perhaps now you gentlemen will understand—and—and give Mr. Ballantine a little time to—to make arrangements," he ended weakly, his voice trailing way as though he were at the end of his physical resources.

"I only understand one thing," said Prufrock drily. "Failing satisfactory assurances as to the Redbury bond issue, which Mr. Ballantine promised to give us here—personally—today, I have my client's instructions to issue a writ against the company. He has failed to keep his appointment—whether, as you seem to suggest, because he has been kidnapped by the person you speak of, or not, does not concern me. Affairs must now take their course. The writ will be served on you on Monday morning. The bank loan, I take it, is being called in at the same time?" He glanced at Robinson, who nodded agreement. "Well, Mr. Du Pine," he continued, "you see the position. We need not occupy your time any further. Good day."

There was no reply. Du Pine, supporting himself by one hand on the table, a lock of his dark hair falling across a forehead glistening with sweat, appeared utterly exhausted. The solicitor shrugged his shoulders, and taking Robinson by the arm walked out of the room without another word.

Du Pine watched them go, and a full minute passed before he roused himself. Then he took from his pocket a small phial of white tablets. This he carried to the lavatory opening out of Ballantine's room. There he filled a glass with water, dropped a tablet in, and watched with eager eyes while it dissolved. He drained the mixture in one gulp and little by little the colour began to come back into his cheeks and the animation to his eyes. When the drug had done its work, he walked back with his usual quick, springy steps, into the room. He took from his pocket a bunch of keys, selected one and fitted it to his employer's private desk. It was all but empty, and of its few contents there were none that interested him. Next he turned his attention to the safe which was let into the wall. Here too his search was fruitless. With a shrug of his shoulders, he cast one last look round the room that had been so long the nerve-centre of a great business, and departed.

3

Mrs. Eales

Mr. Du Pine was quite right. Wherever Ballantine was, he was not with Mrs. Eales. In fact, while Mr. Robinson and Mr. Prufrock were making their enquiries in the City, that lady, sitting up in her bedroom in Mount Street over the remains of a very late breakfast, was wondering earnestly why he was not. A pile of letters lay beside her. They were, and were likely to remain, unopened. Every envelope, she knew, contained a bill, and at the moment she had not the strength of mind that would bear ascertaining how much she owed. In her mind's eye, however, she could not but see some of the items in those bills, and they made her shiver. Her extravagance had in the past been the cause of endless quarrels with her protector, and now, as she glanced at the ominous heap, she automatically reflected: "There'll be a first-class row when he sees that lot." Then, with the dismal realization of how much better was an angry man than no man at all, she felt near to tears.

There was a knock at the door, and before she could answer it, her maid came into the room.

15

"What is it, Florence?" asked Mrs. Eales, with a smile more charming than is usually accorded to their servants by securely placed women.

Florence did not return the smile. Her manner was abrupt—almost insolent.

"Will Mr. Ballantine be coming in today?" she asked.

"I don't know, Florence, I'm sure. Why do you ask?" Then receiving no answer, she went on hastily: "You can have this afternoon off if you want it. I shall be able to manage quite well, even if he does come."

"Thank you, m'm," said Florence, ungraciously. "And can I have my wages for last week, please?"

"Oh, yes, of course, how stupid of me!" cried Mrs. Eales, a thought shrilly. "Fetch my purse from the dressing-table, will you? Now let me see. . . . Oh, dear! I'm so sorry," she exclaimed, fumbling in the purse, "but I seem to have run terribly short. Will it do if I give you ten shillings on account and the rest on Monday?"

Florence took the proffered note without comment, but her eyes rested for a moment on the unopened letters before she went on: "Mr. Du Pine was on the telephone just now."

"Mr. Du Pine!" said Mrs. Eales quickly. "I can't speak to him."

"He didn't want to speak to you. He was just enquiring after Mr. Ballantine. I told him he wasn't here and then he rang off."

"I see. Did he say—did he tell you anything about Mr. Ballantine?"

"No. He just rang up to make sure he wasn't here, he said. He didn't sound as if he thought he would be, somehow."

"That will do, Florence," said her mistress coldly. "Will you take the breakfast things, please?"

16

Florence sulkily removed the tray. At the door she turned, and said over her shoulder:

"If the Captain calls, am I to let him in?"

"Oh, go away, go away!" cried Mrs. Eales, at the end of her patience. The last man in the world of whom she wished to be reminded at that moment was Captain Eales.

4

The Prodigal's Return

Saturday, November 14th

A little before noon a cab drew up outside a small white villa on the outskirts of Passy, and there set down a thin middle-aged man. He was observed and recognized from a first-floor window by a dishevelled maid, who with a *"Tiens!"* of annoyance and surprise set down her feather duster and hastened to make herself presentable before admitting him.

"Bonjour, Eléonore," said John Fanshawe on the threshold, when the door was at length opened to him.

"Monsieur! Mais, que cette arriveé est imprévue!"

"Unexpected, but not unwelcome, I hope," said Fanshawe in French which a long lack of practice had made somewhat uncertain.

Oh, monsieur was joking! As if he could be unwelcome at any time! And had monsieur had a good journey? And was he well? But she could see for herself that he was well—only thin. Mon Dieu! How he was thin! She had hardly known him at first.

"And mademoiselle?" asked Fanshawe, as soon as he could make any headway through the flood of words. "How is she?"

Mademoiselle was well. It was a thousand pities that she was not there to greet her father. If monsieur had but let her know of his approach, how happy she would have been. But it was like monsieur to spring a surprise so happy upon her. And now mademoiselle was out and would not be returned until that afternoon, and nothing was prepared. Monsieur would excuse the confusion in the house, but mademoiselle would of course explain. But what was she—Eléonore—doing? Monsieur was hungry, of course, after his so long journey at this terrible season of the year. Monsieur must eat. There was not much in the house, but an omelette—monsieur would have an omelette *aux fines herbes*, would he not? And some of the Beaujolais wine that he always took with his *déjeuner*? If monsieur would wait but a little quarter of an hour he should be served.

With a final flurry of words she darted away to the kitchen, and Fanshawe with a sigh of relief made his way to the *salon* and sat down to await his meal. His face, which had lit up with pleasure at the well-remembered sound of Eléonore's eloquence, now resumed the expression of wary cynicism that was habitual to him. A mistake, he reflected, to arrive anywhere without warning— even at your own daughter's house. He was old enough to have known better. This was what happened when you had been marking time for years, waiting, concentrating on the one event which would bring you back to life again. You forgot that for the real, live world outside things didn't stand still, as they did for you. He had so often in imagination arrived at this villa to find his daughter on the threshold ready to leap into his arms, that it had not occurred to him that any arrangements were necessary to ensure her being there. A luncheon engagement—an appointment at the hairdresser's—and there was the great reunion scene *manqué*, and the prodigal parent left to eat his omelette alone.

Fanshawe shrugged his lean shoulders. He was making a great fuss about nothing, he told himself. A man comes out of prison a week or so before he is expected to. He visits his daughter in France without warning. Not unnaturally, she is out when he arrives. That was all. But the other half of his intelligence was not so easily satisfied. If that was all, why had Eléonore been so plainly upset at his first appearance? And now, as she appeared with the announcement, "Monsieur est servi!" was there not a trace of pity in the eager friendliness of her manner?

Fanshawe detained her in the dining-room while he ate his lunch. He had had enough of solitude during the last few years. She gossiped with him readily enough about all manner of past acquaintance and happenings, but was reticent on the one subject that interested him at the moment. Once, in a pause in the conversation, she remarked suddenly and apropos of nothing in particular: "Without doubt, mademoiselle will have many things to tell her father."

"*Evidemment*," said Fanshawe in curt agreement, and did not pursue the matter further.

The meal over, he returned to the *salon*, there to smoke and drink the excellent coffee which Eléonore brought him. Tired as he was, he would have slept in his chair, if some part of his consciousness had not remained ceaselessly on the alert, listening for the sound of the front door opening. The lines in his face grew deeper as he waited, and the expression of patient disillusionment more marked.

It was not long before he heard the unmistakable sound of a key being fitted to the door. He rose and took a step towards the hall, then as he heard footsteps hurrying from the interior of the house, returned quietly to his chair. So Eléonore had been on the watch too! The sounds of a whispered colloquy on the doorstep came to his ears, and without hearing what was being said, he realized that for some reason she found it necessary to break the news of his arrival to her mistress. The delay was but a short one, but it seemed long enough to Fanshawe before the door was flung open, and with a cry of "Father!" his daughter was in his arms again.

She quickly broke away from his embrace, and held him at arm's length so that she could see his face, murmuring broken little phrases of concern at his pallor and grey hairs. He on his side looked at her narrowly. She too had changed, he remarked. She had lost some of the girlish charm that he remembered, but in its place had gained the poise and good looks of mature womanhood. "Just the type to attract a Frenchman," he said to himself. Just now her cheeks were flushed, and there was an expression in her eyes which caused him to raise his brows in a mute question.

She noticed it, and by way of answer drew a little further away from him. "I didn't think you would be—be free for another week," she murmured. "I wasn't expecting you."

"I gathered so much from Eléonore."

"Then you didn't get my letter?"

"Evidently not, since I am here. That is, I presume that the letter was to tell me not to come?"

She looked away, in evident distress.

"Father—this is so horribly difficult. . . ."

"Not at all." Fanshawe's dry, unemotional tones were not unkindly. "I am in the way here. That isn't very surprising, is it?"

"Father, you mustn't say that. It sounds so—"

"I can imagine a good many circumstances," he went on, "in which the reappearance of an ex-convict might be embarrassing to his daughter. For example, it might be rather prejudicial to her prospects of a good marriage—"

She drew a sharp breath and looked him in the eyes. He read in her face all that he needed to know.

"We understand each other," he said gravely. "On such occasions, it is the father's duty to disappear as quietly as may be. Only, why didn't you let me know before?"

"I—I tried to, often, but I hadn't the courage. I was a coward, I know, but I kept on putting it off and off until the last moment—I felt so ashamed."

"You have nothing to be ashamed of," he assured her. "Who is the young man? That is, I hope he is young. He is a Frenchman, I suppose?"

"Yes. His name is Paillard—Roger Paillard. He—"

"Of the automobiles Paillard? I congratulate you. And his family, of course, know nothing about me?"

She shook her head. "I am on my way to stay with them for the first time," she said. "He is an only son, and his mother, of course—"

"She, of course, thinks the world of him. And he is *un jeune homme bien élevé, très comme il faut*—and all the rest of it?"

He mimicked the precise accents of an elderly Frenchwoman so well that she laughed in spite of herself.

"Very good," he went on. "I hope you will be happy, my dear. The family skeleton will now return to his cupboard and lock himself in. Where is Roger now, by the way?"

"Outside, in the car. We've been lunching, and I only came in to pick up my bag."

"Then hurry, my dear, hurry. You mustn't keep him waiting! He will be wondering what has become of you."

He kissed her lightly, and she turned to go. At the threshold she stopped.

"What is it?" he asked.

"Father, you never said anything about—I mean, you must be terribly short of money. If I can help—"

"Money?" he echoed her gaily. "No, you needn't worry on that score. We crooks, you know, have always a little nest egg put away somewhere."

She winced at the ugly word, and the ironically defiant tone in which he uttered it.

"But what are you going to do?" she asked.

"Perhaps Eléonore will let me stay the night here," he answered. "Even two nights, if I feel like it. I shall be gone before you return, in any case. Then I shall go back to London. Your aunt has kindly promised to put me up for as long as I please."

"It will be very dull for you," she murmured.

"I don't expect so. And in any case, two lonely people are less dull together than apart. And now you must go. I insist. Good-bye and—good luck."

She left him, and as she ran down the steps to the waiting car, the words "two lonely people" rang in her ears like a tolling bell.

5

Au Café du Soleil

Sunday, November 15th

The Café du Soleil in Goodge Street is always busy at lunch time on Sundays. The narrow white-walled room with its two rows of little tables attracts a clientele from an area far wider than the somewhat shabby neighbourhood that surrounds it. The customers, indeed, are a mixed collection. Many are foreign, some are shabby, a few prosperous, hardly any smart. They are united by one characteristic and one only—that they know and appreciate good food. And Enrico Volpi, the stout little Genoese who learned the art of the kitchen in Marseilles and refined it in Paris, sees that they are not disappointed.

Frank Harper, clerk in the firm of Inglewood, Browne & Company, Auctioneers and Estate Agents of Kensington, had discovered the Soleil in the course of a visit on his employer's business to the Tottenham Court Road. He had been agreeably surprised by the food, and after his meal less agreeably by the bill. Regretfully, as he paid, he had decided that the Soleil was not an eating-house for poor men. He had resolved that so far as he was concerned it must be reserved for some special occasion.

This was such an occasion. Harper had been to a good deal of trouble to plan a meal that should be worthy of it, and Volpi, who knew a young man in love when he saw one, had excelled himself in its execution. So it was with a tone of confidence well justified that over the coffee Harper murmured to his companion:

"Well, Susan, enjoyed your lunch?"

Susan smiled contentedly.

"Frank, it's been the dream of a lunch. I've made a perfect pig of myself, and I shan't be able to eat anything at dinner. You're a perfect genius to have found this place. If only—" Her candid grey eyes had a troubled expression.

"If only—what?"

"If only it wasn't so ruinously expensive."

Harper's rather fatuous expression of happiness gave way to a look of disgust.

"Need you bring that up now?" he asked wearily. "I should have thought—"

Susan was all contrition.

"Darling, I'm sorry. I didn't mean to say anything to spoil things. It was beastly of me."

"Angel, you couldn't be beastly if you tried."

"Yes, I can, and I was. But all the same," she went on, returning to the attack, "we've got to be practical sometimes."

"All right, then," said the young man roughly, "let's be practical. I know what you're thinking. I'm a clerk in a dud firm that pays me two pounds ten shillings a week, which is probably about two pounds nine shillings more than I'm worth. I have been there four years and my prospects of getting any further are precisely nil. You have a dress allowance of fifty pounds a year, and if your

25

father can raise it to a hundred when you're married you will be lucky. Being what are known as gentlefolk, we can't get married under seven hundred a year—say six hundred as a bare minimum. And if we tried it even on that we should hate it, and your father would have seventeen distinct apoplectic fits if we suggested it. Is that practical enough for you?"

"Yes," said Susan in a small sad voice.

"Therefore," he continued, "it ill becomes me to spend fifteen shillings on a decent meal, when I might be putting it in a nice little savings bank, like that ghastly young pup who shares my room at the office."

Susan made a gesture of despair.

"It does seem pretty hopeless, doesn't it?" she said.

Harper looked out past her at the grey prospect of Goodge Street.

"I hate London," he said suddenly.

A silence followed his outburst, and when he spoke again it was in a different tone of voice.

"Susan," he said diffidently, "I've had a letter from a fellow I know out in Kenya. He's got a farm there—sisal, coffee and so on. There's not much money in it nowadays, he says, but it's a good sort of life. If he could take me on—would you come?"

She clapped her hands in joy.

"Darling!" she cried. "But this is marvellous! Why on earth have you kept so quiet about it? You didn't really think I wouldn't come, did you?" Then seeing the irresolute expression on his face, she added: "Frank, there's something else in this. What is it?"

"Yes, there is something else," he answered unwillingly, as though regretting that he had said so much already as to make further disclosure necessary. "There is something else. What this man is offering is a partnership in the farm."

26

"M-m?"

"And he wants fifteen hundred pounds for it."

"O-oh!" Susan's castle in Kenya tumbled in a long drawn sigh of disappointment. "What is the good of talking about things like that? Frank, I thought you were being *practical!*"

He flushed darkly.

"Perhaps I am," he muttered.

"What do you mean? Frank, you make me angry sometimes. You know you haven't got fifteen hundred pounds or the remotest chance of getting it—"

"Suppose I had?"

"What's the good of supposing?" She looked him in the face, and then: "You don't mean—? Darling, I hate mysteries. Are you seriously saying that you can really pay for this partnership, or whatever it is? Tell me."

He smiled at her, though his face was still clouded with anxiety.

"I can't tell you anything now. I'm sorry, darling, but there it is. I've got to see how things work out. But if— just *if*—I came along in a week's time, perhaps less, and told you that the show was on, would you come with me?"

"You know I would!"

"And ask no questions?"

"Why not?"

"And ask no questions, I said."

"Frank, you frighten me when you look like that. It seems so silly. . . . Oh, yes, I suppose so—ask no questions."

"That's all right, then."

She looked at her watch.

"Darling, I must fly, or I shall miss my train, and you know what father is."

She pulled on her close-fitting hat over her mass of

auburn hair and dabbed powder on her nose while Harper paid the bill.

"I wish," she murmured when the waiter had gone, "I wish you could tell me just a little more about it, all the same."

"No, I can't," he answered shortly. "It's just—just something that's happened lately, that's all."

"I don't know what's happened lately," she said as they made their way out. "I tried to read the paper on the way up, but I went to sleep instead. All I saw were some headlines about a Big City Sensation. Has that anything to do with it?"

Harper laughed sardonically.

"In a roundabout way, it might have," he replied, as he pushed open the street door.

On the doorstep Susan almost ran against a small, sallow man who was just coming in. He gave her a look of open admiration of a kind to which she, who was quite aware of her own good looks, was well accustomed. Ordinarily she felt flattered or amused, according to her mood, by these tributes; but for some reason which she could not explain, this man's glance, momentary though it was, filled her with resentment and vague disquiet. She felt as though she were being appraised by a snake.

Meanwhile the new-comer entered the restaurant and seated himself at a table by the window. Whatever the impression he made upon Susan, he was evidently a valued client of the management, for he was no sooner in his place than Volpi, looking like an agitated black water-beetle as he flitted between the tables, came up to him.

"Ah, Monsieur Du Pine!" he cried. "It is a long time since we had the honour. What will monsieur be pleased to take?"

"A *café filtre*," said Du Pine shortly.

Volpi's face fell, but it was not for him to criticize his client's orders, disappointing though they might be. Besides, he too had read the headlines in the newspapers, and he was a man of tact. The coffee was brought with as much ceremony as though it were the most elaborate dish in the menu, and if Volpi had any comments to make they were uttered only to his wife behind the desk.

Du Pine drank his coffee in slow deliberate sips. When it was finished, he lit a cigarette, and that done, another. Little by little the room emptied, but still he showed no signs of leaving. It was almost deserted when at last a man came in and went straight to the vacant seat at his table.

He was of medium height, his thin body clad in a grey suit and overcoat, that had seen better days. Neither his face nor his jerky cock-sparrowlike manner was particularly prepossessing, but there was something in his appearance, whether it was the close-cut sandy moustache or the set of his shoulders, that gave the impression that this had once been an officer—even a gentleman.

Du Pine looked up as he came in. His expression did not change, and when he spoke, only his lips moved.

"You're very late, Eales," he said in a low tone.

"Fog in the Channel," answered Eales shortly. "A double brandy and soda," he added to Volpi, who had appeared at his elbow.

Volpi expressed regret with voice, face and arms.

"Alas, sare, but I am afraid it is too late. These licensing hours—"

"None the less, I think you can get my friend what he wants," put in Du Pine.

"Ah, monsieur must not ask me—"

"But I do ask you," was the cold rejoinder, and the drink was forthcoming immediately.

"I can't think why you wanted me to come to an out-of-the-way hole like this," grumbled Eales as he put down his glass.

"Because it is out of the way. Things have been happening."

"I know that."

"I wonder," said Du Pine with a penetrating stare, "just how much you do know?"

"What do you mean?"

"Do you know, for example, exactly where Ballantine is at this moment?"

"Why should I?"

"Do you know? was my question."

"If it comes to that, do you?"

They looked at each other, mutually suspicious, and then as by common consent looked away.

"We are wasting time," said Du Pine after a short pause. "You haven't told me if your business went off satisfactorily."

"Only because you haven't asked me. In point of fact, it did."

Eales's hand went to his pocket. Du Pine stopped him with a restraining gesture.

"Not here," he murmured. "I have to be rather careful just now. We will do our business in a taxi, if you don't mind. Pay for your drink and we will be off."

Eales displayed his discoloured teeth in a mirthless smile.

"You don't like paying for things, do you, Du Pine?" he remarked.

"I pay for what I get, not otherwise."

In the taxi, Du Pine said affably, "Would you like me to drop you near Mount Street?"

"Why near Mount Street?"

"It occurred to me that Mrs. Eales might be glad of your company just now."

"You can leave my wife out of it, blast you!" said Eales violently.

"Just as you please. Now next time—"

"There isn't going to be a next time!"

"All the same, I think there is," said Du Pine softly.

6

Not in the Inventory

"Mr. Harper?"

"Yes, Mr. Brown."

"I want your attention, please. And yours too, Mr. Lewis."

"Very good, sir."

Harper put down the pencil with which he had been playing, and looked with disgust at his fellow employee. Not for the world would he have allowed himself to call Mr. Browne "sir". Lewis saw the glance and scowled in reply. In every respect but their age and occupation the two young men were utterly dissimilar, and for various reasons they disliked each other cordially. Harper was slim, dark and sharp-featured. Lewis was pug-nosed, fair and heavily built. Lewis took his position and duties seriously. He was satisfied with his employment, which had come to him as the result of much hard labour at night classes and correspondence schools during long years of drudgery as an office boy. His ambition was to qualify himself as an <u>auctioneer, surveyor</u> and <u>estate agent</u>, and his horizon was bounded by a partnership in Inglewood,

Browne & Co. Harper, on the contrary, considered himself thoroughly ill-treated by the fate which had thrown him abruptly out of Oxford into what he felt to be an unworthy occupation, and somewhat foolishly, he made no secret of the fact. He could not be induced to look upon his job as anything but a disagreeable necessity, and therefore treated it with a casualness that, combined with his indefinable and quite unintentional air of superiority, caused Lewis perpetual annoyance. In consequence, they avoided each other as much as was reasonably possible, but in a small office they were continually being thrown together and therefore continually jarring on each other.

"No. 27 Daylesford Gardens," said Mr. Browne. He cleared his throat pompously. "Furnished letting, Miss Penrose to—to—er—"

"Colin James."

"Thank you, Mr. Harper. To Mr. Colin James. For four weeks, expiring tomorrow. The tenant appears to have vacated the premises before the end of the lease. It is none the less our duty to protect our client's interests to—ah—the best of our ability. Mr. Harper?"

"Yes, Mr. Browne."

"You will please take Miss Penrose's copy of the inventory of contents and check it carefully—*carefully* with—ah—with the contents. You understand?"

"Perfectly."

"Making at the same time a careful note of any dilapidations which you may—which you may note."

"Quite."

"Mr. Lewis?"

"Yes, sir."

"You will go along with Mr. Harper, and supervise him."

"Very good, sir."

"Really, Mr. Browne," Harper protested, "I think I am quite capable of doing a simple job like that without any assistance."

"You may think so, Mr. Harper. Unfortunately, I do not. I have observed recently a certain regrettable—ah—laxity in your work. It is most undesirable in our class of business that we should be in any way—ah—lax. That is why I consider it necessary to send you to check the inventory, and Mr. Lewis to check *you*."

With a faint snigger at his own attempted witticism Mr. Browne thereupon withdrew to his private office.

The two young men walked to Daylesford Gardens in thoroughly bad tempers. Harper had many reasons for feeling annoyed, among them the slight which had been put upon him and the consciousness that it was quite justified. Lewis, on his side, while pleased that the superior Harper had been "taken down a peg", disliked being sent out on an unnecessary errand.

At the door, Lewis broke the silence in which they had walked together from the office.

"Have you got the key?" he asked.

"It would have been rather more useful if you had asked that question before we started," replied Harper coldly. "As a matter of fact, I have."

They passed inside.

"Have you got the inventory?" said Lewis.

This time Harper made no attempt to reply. He merely pulled a folded paper from his pocket and planted himself with his back to the door.

"You read them out and I'll check them off," said Lewis.

Harper shrugged his shoulders wearily, and in a tone of infinite disgust began to read: "Hall and passage. Five and a half yards green lino . . ."

"Right."

34

"Carved mahogany hat-stand. . . . God, why do people have such things?"

"Right."

"Ebony-framed wall mirror. . . . ."

"Right. No, it isn't. One corner's badly chipped."

"Well, it doesn't say so here."

"Then it's a dilapidation. Mark it down."

Harper made a note. "Not that it'll do much good to anybody," he said, "as the tenant has gone abroad."

"He had no call to go until he'd settled the dilapidations," snapped Lewis. "Anyhow, we must protect our client. She's got a right to claim for it. Put it down."

"Oh, by all means," said Harper in his most infuriating manner. "Shall we proceed? Japanese lacquer hanging cupboard. . . ."

The hall completed, they passed to the front room on the ground floor. It was not a large room, but grossly over-furnished, and checking its contents proved a long and laborious affair. Lewis found two further small dilapidations and a cheap brass ashtray which was not in the inventory, and gloated audibly at his own perspicacity. Harper's impatience became more and more manifest until at last his companion's conscientiousness was satisfied and allowed him to move on to the smoking-room.

Harper was the first through the door. He stopped in the entrance, and as Lewis was about to follow, held him back.

"Just a moment," he said gently. "I think there's something here that isn't in the inventory."

The telephone bell rang in the police station which was at the corner of Upper Daylesford Street and the Fulham Road. Sergeant Tapper, who was a conscientious officer, made a note of the time before he answered

35

it. It was 11.31 A.M. He put the receiver to his ear, and at first could make nothing of the message. He heard a succession of gasps, as if the speaker had been running fast. Finally a thick voice exclaimed: "Murder, murder! Come at once!"

"What do you say?" barked Tapper. "Who are you? Where—?"

"I say there's been a murder—" repeated the voice. There was a moment's silence, and the sergeant thought he had been cut off. Then a quiet, cultured voice broke in:

"I'm speaking from 27 Daylesford Gardens. Mr. Lionel Ballantine's body is here. Will you come and remove it, please? . . . Yes, certainly I'll wait for you. Good-bye."

Tapper leapt from his chair with a speed that would have been remarkable in a younger man. Within a bare half-minute of putting down the receiver he was out of the police station, a young constable at his heels, while at the telephone another officer sent an urgent message to Scotland Yard.

At the door of No. 27 the officers found the two young men awaiting them. Both had the appearance of having recently been through an unpleasant experience. Of the two, Harper was noticeably the cooler. It was he who greeted Tapper.

"Glad to see you, sergeant," he said. "You will find him in the room at the back. Nothing has been touched."

They followed the policeman through the hall into the smoking-room. The blind was down and the electric light burning. The contrast to the light of day outside gave a touch of unreality to the scene. There was a moment's silence, as all gazed at the corpse. Here was no dignity in death, no repose. The sprawled, stiffened figure was like a monstrous marionette, hideous, grotesque, unseemly.

The sergeant bent over the remains for an instant, then straightened himself.

"The divisional surgeon will be here in a minute or two, I expect," he said. "Not that there will be much for him to do, it seems. Then I'm expecting a senior officer from the Yard. You can keep your full statements for him. Meanwhile I'll just take down a few particulars." He produced his notebook. "Names and addresses, please," he began, and, these transcribed, continued: "Which of you was it that telephoned?"

"I did," answered Harper. "That is, mine was, I think, the effective message. My friend here actually had the first words, but I don't think they carried very much weight."

Lewis went an angry red. "We're not all of us used to finding bodies about the place," he muttered.

"That's all right, me lad," said Tapper kindly. "Nobody's going to blame you for being a bit upset at a nasty sight like that. It's only natural." He turned to Harper. "And how did you know this was Mr. Ballantine?" he demanded.

For reply, Harper took a newspaper from his pocket.

"Fairly obvious, wasn't it?" he remarked.

A streamer headline across the front page shouted in large capitals: "RIDDLE OF MISSING FINANCIER: WHERE IS MR. BALLANTINE?" Beneath it was a photograph of a man in early middle age, with a prosperous, conceited, not unhandsome face, dressed in a morning coat, grey top-hat and stock, an orchid in his buttonhole. The caption ran: "Mr. Lionel Ballantine; a photo taken at this year's Derby."

The sergeant looked from the photograph to the distorted face of the murdered man, and back again. "That's him all right, I can see that," he said.

He pursed his lips and remained silent for a moment.

"What were you two doing here?" he asked.

"Checking the inventory for the leaseholder, Miss Penrose," put in Lewis, who felt it was time to assert himself. "She had let this place furnished and—"

"She hadn't let it to Mr. Ballantine, I suppose?" asked Tapper.

"Lord, no! The tenant was a Mr. James. Sergeant, do you think—?"

"I think you two had better get on with your job of checking the inventory," said Tapper. "We shall know then if anything's missing from the house, at all events, and by the time you've finished I expect there will be someone here from the Yard to hear what you've got to say. Be careful, now. Nothing's to be touched; and if you find anything suspicious, call me at once."

The young men left the room obviously relieved to be able to get away from it and the atmosphere of violence and horror that pervaded it. The sergeant, after posting the constable at the front door to warn off any intruders, pulled out his notebook and pencil and began to make laborious notes in his round, board-school handwriting. Presently he was interrupted by the arrival of an officer from the police station, who brought with him the divisional surgeon. The latter, a pale little man with a reddish moustache, took little time over his examination.

"Strangulation," he said briefly.

"How long has he been dead?" asked Tapper.

"It's difficult to say—two or three days, approximately."

"Well, we shall have to wait for further orders before we move him. Then perhaps you'll be able to tell us something further."

"A message from the Yard has just come through," put in the newly arrived constable. "Inspector Mallett is coming down immediately. Meanwhile nothing is to be touched."

"Does he think I don't know my own business?" grumbled Tapper. "You can get along back to the station, me lad, and if you meet any newspaper men on the doorstep, keep your mouth shut."

By way of protest he put away his notebook, as though determined that the too officious Mallett should have no further help from him. Consequently, he at once found himself with nothing to do. The surgeon rolled a cigarette and inserted it in a long holder, and settling down in a chair began to smoke with an air of melancholy boredom. Tapper tried to engage him in conversation, but found him little more communicative than Mr. Ballantine would have been. Finally, casting about for something to occupy his mind, he picked up the newspaper which Harper had left behind, and set himself to read the letterpress which straggled above, below and round-about the photographs of Mr. Lionel Ballantine and of the ornate façade of his London offices.

It was a mixture of fact and comment. The facts were brief, for the obvious reason that none were known beyond the all-important one that Mr. Ballantine, leaving his office at the usual time on Friday afternoon, had not been seen up to a late hour on Sunday night, although a large number of persons were extremely anxious to see him. The comment, on the other hand, was voluminous and pointed. It was couched in the careful style that is usually adopted by the press in relation to a man whose prosecution is to be expected but is not yet inevitable. It was artistically contrived to leave every reader under the firm impression that the object of its attention was a fugitive from justice, while cautiously abstaining from anything that might conceivably go beyond the bounds set by the law of libel. Mr. Lionel Ballantine, the newspaper reminded its readers, had for many years been an important figure in the City of London. He was in particular the chairman of the London and Imperial Estates Company, Ltd., a concern with an issued capital of two and a half million pounds. The article went on to remind its readers that the shares in the company, after having made what in a happy turn of phrase it described as a meteoric rise during the early part of the year, had collapsed abruptly in the past few days and were now quoted at one-tenth of their nominal value. The City, it added sagely, was gravely perturbed at the turn of events and the annual report and balance sheet, due in a fortnight's time, were anxiously awaited. It went on to hint vaguely at repercussions and developments that might be expected. In conclusion, the writer remarked with an air of detachment that would not have deceived a child that it would be recollected that Mr. Ballantine's name had been mentioned at the sensational trial of John Fanshawe over four years previously.

The sergeant looked up from his reading.

"Fanshawe!" he said aloud.

"Eh?" said the surgeon, spilling his cigarette ash on the carpet.

"He was released from Maidstone the other day, wasn't he?"

"Thursday."

"Fanshawe out and Ballantine dead," mused Tapper. "Quite a coincidence, you might say. Wasn't Ballantine supposed to have been mixed up in the Fanshawe bank fraud?"

But the surgeon's interest in the subject seemed to have been already exhausted. Tapper sighed and turned to the football forecasts.

7

Inspector Mallett

Lewis and Harper, their work above stairs completed, descended to a ground floor that seemed suddenly to have become crowded with people. Heavy police boots tramped in the hall, and through the smoking-room door they could see the sudden flash of magnesium as photographers recorded the appearance of the room and its occupant. Scotland Yard had taken possession.

Sergeant Tapper met them at the foot of the stairs.

"The inspector wants a word with you," he said.

Inspector Mallett was a tall, stout man, whose bulk, as he stood four-square in the middle of the carpet, seemed to make the small room still smaller. From a rosy, round face looked out bland blue eyes, the mild expression of which contrasted oddly with his fierce military moustache. He favoured the two young men with a quiet, appraising stare as they entered.

"These are the two men who—" began Tapper.

"Yes," said Mallett. He turned at once to Harper. "Have you finished with your inventory?" he asked.

"Yes," answered Harper. "Every room except this one, of course."

"Then just run your eye over this room, and tell me if anything has been taken."

Harper began to go through the list, checking it off with the objects in the room. Not for the world would he, in this room, and in the presence of all these strangers, acknowledge the need of Lewis's help. Lewis, on his part, was equally determined to see that the job was done thoroughly, and to Harper's extreme annoyance, took up a position at his elbow where he could look over the inventory and correct what was being done. As quickly as possible Harper completed the work, a desire to be out of the room and to be away from his companion spurring him on.

"There's nothing missing," he announced.

"Yes, there is," said the odious Lewis in the same breath. "The blind-cord has gone."

Harper could not avoid showing his annoyance at his own lapse and his contempt for the other's uncalled-for nicety; but the inspector smiled grimly.

"Is this it, do you think?" he asked, pointing to the dead man.

Both had hitherto averted their eyes from the grisly object in the chair as much as possible, while taking in everything above, below and around it, but now, following the direction of the detective's pointing finger, they saw protruding from the back of the neck, just above the collar, an unmistakable wooden knob, attached to a thin cord, most of it so embedded in the folds of the skin as to be invisible. Speechless, they nodded in agreement.

"Right!" said Mallett cheerfully. "That's one thing settled, anyway. Now I don't expect you fellows want to be in here any longer than you can help. Come into the other room."

He consulted in low tones with one of his subordinates before leading the way into the front room. While he did so, Harper, his repugnance now conquered by curiosity, gazed with close interest at the face of the dead man. The body had been moved for the photographers to do their work, and it was possible for him now to look at the upturned features more closely. There was no trace of sympathy in the young man's expression as he stared, but only a deep interest. It seemed unnatural that one who had probably never seen death before, and certainly not in such terrible guise, should be able to regard it with such passionless curiosity. So absorbed was he that he was evidently unaware that he too was the object of scrutiny from eyes no less observant than his own.

"Well?" said Mallett's voice suddenly close behind him. "What are you staring at?"

Harper started, and it was an appreciable time before he could recover his self-possession. When he did speak, however, it was in his airiest and most superior tone. Lewis, listening, privately concluded that he had decided to assume his Oxford manner so as to impress upon the inspector that he was something more than an ordinary estate agent's clerk.

"As a matter of fact, Inspector," he said, "I was wondering why an obviously well-dressed man like that should have chosen to wear a green bow tie with a grey suit."

The inspector grunted, but said nothing.

"Particularly", pursued Harper, "when it isn't even decently tied. I shouldn't like to be seen dead in it myself."

"Probably Ballantine wouldn't either," snapped Mallett. "If you've finished with the camera, cover that up, one of you, until it can be moved." He strode out of the room, motioning the two young men to follow him.

"I shan't keep you long," said the inspector, when they were alone together. "I know who you are and why you were here. Just let me have a few details about the house. Whose is it?"

"Miss Penrose's," said Harper. "She is a client of ours, and is in Italy for the winter."

"That is," put in Lewis heavily, "Miss Penrose is the leaseholder. Actually the house belongs to Lord Minfield."

"We won't bother about him," said Mallett. "Then you let it furnished on Miss Penrose's behalf?"

"Yes," said Harper.

"For how long?"

"A month, expiring today."

"What was the tenant's name?"

"Colin James."

"Where is he now?"

"Abroad, so far as I know," said Harper. "That is, on Saturday morning he returned the keys of the house with a letter to say that he was giving up possession and going to France."

"What do you know about him?" asked Mallett. "He gave you some references, I suppose?"

"The only reference he gave was his bank," said Harper. "He paid the rent in advance."

"Which bank was it?"

"The Southern—the Lower Daylesford Street branch. I remember that because it was the same as the firm's."

The detective paused for a moment, sucking his cheeks reflectively, his broad back to the window, through which came the murmur of a crowd, already collected at the signs of police activity.

"What did this Colin James look like?" was his next question.

"He was a fat man," answered Harper, "or rather, paunchy. I mean, he had a big stomach and a thin face, as if he had a bad digestion. He had a rather large dark brown beard. He was about medium size, and as far as I can remember, he spoke in rather a husky voice."

Mallett turned to Lewis. "Do you agree with that?" he asked.

"I never saw him," said Lewis. "I only came in on this job because Mr. Browne, my boss, wanted me to help check the inventory." He could not resist a spiteful glance at Harper as he spoke.

"In that case you needn't wait here," said Mallett. "Get back to your office, tell them what has happened, if they don't know already, and ask them to have all their records about Mr. James and his tenancy ready for inspection. I'll let you know when you're wanted again. Not until the inquest, probably."

Lewis left, and the inspector turned to Harper.

"How often did you see James?" he asked.

"Only once. He came into the office in the morning when I was alone, and said he wanted a quiet furnished house in a hurry. I took him out and showed him this place—"

"Leaving the office empty?"

"Mr. Browne was in the inner office, but wouldn't see him from where he was."

"I see. Go on."

"He liked the look of it and wanted to move in that afternoon. I took him back to the office and he gave me his cheque, which I paid into the bank during the morning. In the afternoon, Mr. Browne made out the tenancy agreement, and later on in the day Mr. James came back and signed it."

"Were you alone in the office then?"

"Yes. As a matter of fact—everyone else had gone home, and I had to wait specially late for him."

"The tenancy agreement will be in the office, I suppose?"

Harper appeared to hesitate. "Yes—I suppose so," he said. "It should be, at any rate."

"You've given a very good description of a man you only saw once," Mallett pursued. "Had you any particular reason for remembering him?"

"No—I don't think so. Except of course a beard is a bit unusual."

"Quite. Would you know him again if you were to see him?"

"I think so—only there's the beard again. I'm not sure if I should know him without that."

The inspector nodded thoughtfully.

"Was he alone in the house, do you know?" he asked. "It seems a biggish place for one man to take."

"So far as I know he was."

"What about servants?"

"He said he would want a man to come in by the day. I engaged one for him."

"What is his name?"

"Crabtree—Richard Crabtree. He lives in the Terrace, just round the corner. No. 14."

"Thank you," said Mallett, making a note of the address. "Now about this inventory. Is there anything missing from the house?"

"No—nothing of any consequence."

"Anything may be of consequence in a case like this," said Mallett severely. "You had better leave the list with me for reference. Is there anything here that isn't on it?"

"Only the linen and cutlery which James brought in with him."

46

"That may be important. Where did it come from?"

"I ordered it myself for him from the stores near our office, and he gave me the money when he called to sign the agreement."

"Rather an unusual transaction for a house agent to do, wasn't it?"

"Yes, I suppose it was," admitted Harper. "But he asked me to do it, and I didn't think of it at the time."

"I see." Mallett went to the door. The interview was evidently at an end, and Harper rose to go. But the detective stopped him.

"Just one more question," he said. "Have you ever seen Ballantine before?"

"No."

"Then what exactly was it that made you stare at him in the way you did just now?"

"Exactly what I told you," answered Harper coldly.

"No more than that?"

"No."

The inspector shrugged his shoulders. "Very well. I shall keep in touch with you and let you know when you are wanted again. Good day."

He opened the door, and Harper stepped into the open air again. He was conscious of the sound of many voices, of the click of cameras, of the hot breath of a crowd surging round him. But in his relief to be free at last of the horrors of the morning he gave them no heed. Pushing his way through, he walked at his best pace to the end of the street. Then he suddenly realized that he was very tired and distinctly hungry. Looking at his watch, he was astonished to find that it was not yet one o'clock. In an hour and a half he had lived an age. From the window, Inspector Mallett, with a quizzical expression on his lips and a slight frown barring his broad forehead, watched him go.

47

8

Richard Crabtree

Tuesday, November 17th

If the disappearance of Lionel Ballantine had been front-page news in the morning papers, his reappearance as a corpse in an obscure South Kensington house was a sensation of the first magnitude. It occupied the posters of every news-sheet in London, quite excluding such minor matters as a Cabinet crisis, a film star's divorce and an earthquake in China. From morning till night a throng of morbid sight-seers blocked the pavement of Daylesford Gardens, to the disgust of its retired but still surviving inhabitants, and gazed with hungry rapture at the commonplace exterior of No. 27. When they finally returned home they were able to feast their eyes on faithful photographs of the same view. One photographer, more enterprising than the rest, had been able to penetrate to the back, and thence to secure a picture of the window of the actual room where the dead man had been found. His effort was rightly considered to be quite a scoop by his paper, which further assisted its readers by marking the particular window with a cross.

The police had been chary in the details which they issued for publication, but news editors and special reporters were not slow to make the most of the material available. Everybody who could conceivably have had any knowledge of the tragedy, not to mention a great many who could not, was pestered by interviewers. Mrs. Brent's particular friend, making a quiet and quick getaway from No. 34, had the fright of his life when he was held up just outside the house by a determined young man whom he took to be an enquiry agent, but who was in fact merely a reporter thirsting for a personal story from a resident. Jackie Roach, on the other hand, thoroughly enjoyed himself. Not only did the murder, as he had foretold, stimulate his sales, but for the first and last time in his life, he was himself part of the news he sold. To be shouting: "Special! Murder! All the latest!"—to be thrusting into eager hands papers with your own picture on the front page—to be photographed in the act of doing so by another pressman— to know that that picture would be in tomorrow's paper, and that tomorrow you might be photographed selling a paper with a picture of yourself—it all fairly went to a chap's head, more even than the drinks which those reporters kept on standing you every time you thought of something extra for them to put in the story.

Roach had of course given his statement to the police and been warned that he must attend the inquest. In the meantime, he had been told to keep his mouth shut. But it wasn't in human nature to keep one's mouth shut when there were so many temptations to open it for the admission of free beer, and Jackie was too honest a man not to do his best to give value for his entertainment. It was wonderful, too, what questions they thought of asking. Things that the police had never bothered him about. For instance, he just happened to mention that he knew Crabtree, Mr. James's servant, and they fairly buzzed with excitement. When had he seen him last? Where was he now? Jackie was blest if he knew. But his very ignorance, it seemed, was news enough, and on the morning after the discovery of Ballantine's death, "WHERE IS RICHARD CRABTREE?" was a question which was worth a headline to itself in some newspapers.

Crabtree, in fact, about the time that these same papers were being read at countless breakfast tables throughout the country, was standing rather forlornly in the main street of Spellsborough, a small market town in Sussex. At his back was a gaunt ugly building with the words "County Police" on the lamp over its main entrance. Across the road, in the direction in which he was looking, was a garage, where a heavy motor lorry had just pulled up to refuel, and towards this he directed a look of hopeful interest.

The lorry driver paid for his petrol, cranked the engine and climbed up into his seat. As he did so, Crabtree crossed the road and came up on his near side.

"Going to London, mate?" he asked.

The driver was a pale-faced, fleshy man with a permanent frown of discontent. He looked down at Crabtree with eyes that seemed to twinkle with malice.

"Ye're just out o' the lock-up, ain't yer?" he said, jerking his thumb at the building across the road.

"What's that got to do with you?" said Crabtree defensively.

"That's all right," was the answer. "I've suffered from the so-called justice of the ruling classes meself. We of the proletariat 'ave got to stick together. Jump in, comrade. Ye're welcome to a lift to London—if this perishing box o' tricks will get so far."

He crashed the engine into gear and the lorry crawled slowly up the steep street and on to the open downs beyond.

"In Soviet Russia", observed the driver, "the output of motor trucks 'as increased three 'undred per cent in the last five years. That makes yer think a bit, don't it?"

Crabtree, who, if he thought at all, was not accustomed to think of such subjects, contented himself with a noncommittal grunt. They continued to drive in silence for several miles before his companion spoke again.

"If yer don't believe me," he said, as though the one-sided conversation had never been interrupted, "just take a look at this." He pulled a newspaper from his pocket. "*The Daily Toiler*," he added with reverence in his voice. "Yer can believe what yer reads in the *Toiler*. It's the truth, comrade—not just lying capitalist progaganda, like some I could mention."

An emphatic spit over the side emphasized his contempt for the lords of Fleet Street.

Crabtree took the paper, and glanced without much attention at the small print to which the driver's grubby fingei pointed. The statistics of the special correspondent in Moscow promised little entertainment, and it was not long before he turned to the front page. What he saw there interested him a good deal more. Whatever the differences between *The Daily Toiler* and its capitalist competitors, its standard of news values was fundamentally the same. Politics may differ, but a murder is a murder all the world over.

" 'Ere, 'ullo! What's this?" he exclaimed.

"That? One of these blarsted millionaires gone to 'is account," said the driver with gloomy relish. "And serve 'im right, I say! Bloodsuckers, every one of 'em! Each for 'imself and the weakest goes to the wall—that's capitalism for yer!"

He swung the heavy vehicle round a bend, forcing a cyclist into the hedge. Crabtree, hanging on with difficulty, neither saw nor heard. His whole attention was focused on the printed words before him.

"Twenty-seven Daylesford Gardens!" he murmured incredulously.

He read with difficulty, the words dancing up and down before his eyes to the jolting of the road. Then he saw something which almost caused him to tumble from his seat. From the mass of print one name stood out in heavy, accusing capitals—his own.

" 'Strewth!" said Crabtree.

He was still staring at the paper in incredulous dismay when the lorry pulled up with a jerk. Looking up, he saw that they were on the crest of a steep hill. From the radiator cap came a thin jet of steam. The driver switched off the engine.

"Boiling again, as per usual," he announced philosophically. "Now we'll just 'ave to wait till 'er 'ighness is pleased to cool off. What's the matter, comrade?"

Crabtree handed him over *The Daily Toiler*.

"Just look at that there," he said. "Twenty-seven Daylesford Gardens—where I was in service. Colin James—the gent I was doing for. And me—the blighters have got me in it too!"

The driver studied the page for some time in silence. Then he took a cigarette from behind his ear and lit it.

"The perlice are anxious to interview", he quoted, "Richard Crabtree. That you?"

"Yes, that's me all right, mate, but—"

"Ar!" He pondered in silence for a while, and then:

"The perlice, indeed! Well, sooner you than me. We'd best be getting on."

A few hundred yards farther on the road crossed a small stream. Here he stopped the machine again, and produced a small tin jug, which he handed to Crabtree.

"Just get down and fill 'er up with water, will yer, comrade?" he said.

Crabtree was down at the waterside when he heard the roar of the engine being accelerated. He ran back just in time to see the lorry mount the bridge and disappear in a cloud of exhaust smoke. A voice floated back to his ears:

"I don't want no dealings with the perlice, thank you, comrade!"

It had begun to rain. He was five miles from the nearest village, and his only possession in the world was an empty half-gallon tin jug.

9

Inquest on a Financier

Wednesday, November 18th

"The inquest will be held on Wednesday." This simple statement, which concluded every newspaper account of the mystery of Daylesford Gardens, had at least the merit of being accurate and readily understood. Not unnaturally, those of the public who had time on their hands regarded it as an invitation to be present at what promised to be a sensational enquiry. The niggardly spirit in which the architect had interpreted his duty when designing the court made this invitation a useless one to nine out of ten of those who endeavoured to accept it; but with a truly British determination they continued to skirmish outside the doors long after the last hope was gone.

On Wednesday morning, therefore, the coroner took his seat in a court which was crowded to suffocation. Inspector Mallett sat close at hand, his moustache bristling with disgust at the jostling mob of sensation-hunters. He disliked inquests. They did no good, he considered, and only wasted time which might have been spent in more profitable ways. Still, they were part of the machinery of the law, of which he was the servant, and as such he accepted them with resignation. Their only useful function, in his experience, was to focus public attention on a case, and so to induce witnesses to come forward who otherwise would have remained in ignorance of the value of their evidence; and on this case, he reflected, blowing out his cheeks in the already vitiated atmosphere, there had already been public attention enough and to spare. Fortunately, he knew this coroner to be an amenable individual, who would not do more than discharge the necessary duties of his office, without pushing the enquiry further than he, Mallett, thought necessary at this stage.

The proceedings were opened and the coroner briefly addressed the jury. They were met, he told them, to enquire into the death of Mr. Lionel Ballantine. Certain evidence would be put before them from which it would be clear that the deceased had met with an unnatural death. It was impossible for them in the present state of the investigations to complete their enquiry, and an adjournment would be necessary to give time for the police to clear the matter up fully. It would depend upon the result of the work of the police, he added, whether or not it would be his duty to call the jury together again.

"That means, whether they catch the man or not," whispered Lewis knowingly. Harper, sitting reluctantly at his side, felt slightly sick. But his attention was soon diverted as the evidence began.

"Mrs. Ballantine," cried the coroner's officer, and a slender figure in black stepped forward. Those in the witnesses' seats near the front of the court could discern a composed face, level brows and a thin, inflexible mouth.

"You are Evangeline Mary Ballantine?" asked the coroner.

"Yes."

55

"And you live at 59 Belgrave Square?"

"Yes."

"Have you identified the body of your husband, shown to you in the mortuary at this court?"

"I have."

"When did you last see your husband alive?"

"Last Wednesday—a week ago today."

"Was he then in his usual health?"

"So far as I could see—yes."

The coroner consulted the papers before him, cleared his throat, and went on in a slightly different tone.

"You and your husband were not living together, I think?"

"We were not formally separated," said Mrs. Ballantine in a voice from which all expression seemed deliberately excluded. "My house was open to him whenever he cared to use it."

"And did he use it, from time to time?"

"From time to time—yes. I cannot say exactly how often. It is a large house, and I did not question him him as to his movements."

"On this occasion, a week ago, did you see him at Belgrave Square?"

"Yes, I asked him to come and see me. I had to discuss money matters with him."

"Did—?" the coroner began another question, but thought better of it. Instead he turned to the barrister who represented Mrs. Ballantine.

"Have you any questions?" he asked.

Counsel had only one question. "Did your husband ever mention to you the address, 27 Daylesford Gardens?"

"No."

He turned to the coroner. "Will this witness be required any longer?" he asked. "If not, she would be obliged if—"

"By all means," was the answer. "She may go at once."

Counsel sat down with the easy conscience of one who has earned his fee, and Mrs. Ballantine nodded her thanks to the coroner and turned to go, as composed as she had come. Neither then nor at any time did she display any sign of emotion. She passed through the throng as though it had not been there and was gone. Mallett was not an impressionable man, but as she left the court he found his eyes following her with admiration and respect. "A hard nut, that woman," he thought. "No wonder Ballantine went elsewhere for his fun! But she's got character—and courage. A woman like that would do—anything!"

The police surgeon was the next witness. He brought an air of businesslike efficiency into the court, giving his evidence with a matter-of-fact taciturnity that made it seem positively ordinary. Many of his audience, agape for thrills, felt that they had been in some way cheated. Later in the day, when they opened their evening papers and read the same evidence in all the glory of headlines and leaded type, they were able to recapture the sensations and the drama which had been so oddly missing in the original.

The surgeon briskly gave his name, address and qualifications. He had been called to 27 Daylesford Gardens. There he had seen the body of the deceased. Rigor mortis had already set in. It was impossible to say accurately how long he had been dead, but he estimated from two to three days. That would place the time of death between midday on Friday and midday on Saturday. If anything, he thought it would be rather towards the beginning of that period. Asked specifically whether appearances were consistent with death on Friday afternoon or evening, he agreed that that was so.

"Did you find anything to account for the death?" asked the coroner.

"Yes—a thin piece of cord was passed twice round the neck and tightly knotted at the back."

"Was this the piece of cord in question?"

For the first time in his recital there was a stir of interest in court, as an impassive officer placed the exhibit before the witness. The surgeon glanced at it, said "Yes", and plunged into medical details. He had conducted a post-mortem. The body was healthy and well nourished. There was no trace of organic disease. Death was due to strangulation. Great force must have been used, suicide was out of the question. He gathered up his papers and left the box with the same air of dreary efficiency that he had displayed throughout.

Harper and then Lewis were next called to give their account of the finding of the body. The inspector, listening idly to what was for him a twice-told tale, took a certain grim amusement in noting the difference in their attitude. Harper was before the coroner as he had been to the detective, aloof, detached and cool; Lewis, on the contrary, was flustered and excited. He evidently took a vulgar delight in being for once the centre of interest, and was much more concerned to describe his own sentiments of horror and amazement at what he saw than to add anything useful to the enquiry. He had already, Mallett knew, allowed himself to be interviewed and photographed by press reporters, unlike Harper, who had done all in his power to avoid publicity. Altogether the pair made a contrast which to a psychologist— and every good detective must be something of a psychologist—was not without interest, and, possibly, profit.

The coroner looked at the clock. He had been satisfactorily expeditious so far, and he was anxious to finish the case before lunch.

"There are only two more witnesses," he told the jury. "We will deal with them now."

The jury, aching on hard wooden benches, and longing to escape from the fetid air, wriggled impatiently but made no protest.

"Mr. Du Pine," called the coroner's officer.

Du Pine, looking haggard and careworn, came forward.

He took the oath in a nervous fashion, holding the Testament as though he were afraid it would bite him, and breathed deeply two or three times before he answered the questions put to him.

"Your name is Hector Du Pine?" asked the coroner.

"Yes."

"And do you live at 92 Fitz-James Avenue, St. John's Wood?"

"I do."

"Are you the secretary of the London and Imperial Estates Company?"

"Yes—that is—yes, I am."

"Of which the deceased was the chairman?"

Mr. Du Pine cleared his throat, bared his teeth in a nervous grin, and sighed rather than said: "He was."

"When did you last see the deceased?"

"About five o'clock in the afternoon of last Friday."

"Was that at the offices of the London and Imperial Estates Company?"

"Yes, I should say," Mr. Du Pine hastened to correct himself, "it was just outside the offices. On the pavement."

"You were outside the offices on the pavement with him?"

"No. I was inside, at my window."

"You were watching out of your window and saw him go?"

"Just so."

"Did you see which way he went?"

"No, I don't think I did . . . No, decidedly no."

"You had no particular reason for watching, I suppose?" suggested the coroner.

Mr. Du Pine's eyelids flickered once or twice before he answered: "No—no particular reason."

"Was he alone then?"

"He was."

"Had he anything with him?"

"Just an umbrella—nothing else."

"Had you been talking to him before he left?"

"Oh, yes—just before."

"And did he seem in normal health and spirits then?"

"Quite normal, so far as his health went," answered the secretary. Then in lowered tones he added: "He was, of course, rather worried about business matters."

"And I suppose he had been discussing these business matters with you?"

"Yes. Oh, yes, he had."

"Did he tell you where he was going when he left?"

"No. Oh, no. He was not—not a very communicative man, apart from business."

"Did he ever mention No. 27 Daylesford Gardens to you at any time?"

"Certainly not."

"Thank you," said the coroner, with a nod of dismissal. But Mr. Du Pine had still something to say.

"I think I ought to mention," he said breathlessly, his thin hands clutching the rail of the witness-box as though he were afraid he might be forcibly removed before he had finished, "I might say, that Mr. Ballantine had expressed himself that morning as being very much concerned, alarmed indeed—"

"About business matters. You have told us that already," interjected the coroner.

"No, not about business," persisted the witness, "there was that, of course, as well. But I mean he seemed to be alarmed in a personal way."

"As to his safety, do you mean?"

"Yes."

"Did he tell you the cause of this alarm you speak of?"

Du Pine swallowed twice before he spoke. "He had had a visitor that morning", he said hurriedly, "who seemed to—to have disturbed him very much indeed. He left strict instructions that he should not be admitted again."

There was a stir in the audience at this evidently completely unexpected piece of evidence. Mallett pursed his lips and frowned. But the coroner could not leave the matter there.

"Did he give the name of his visitor?" he asked.

"Yes—he did." The witness seemed indisposed to say more.

"What was the name?"

"John Fanshawe." The words were muttered rather than spoken, but in the tense silence they reached every corner of the court. They were greeted with an excited murmur, instantly followed by a stentorian cry of "Silence, silence!" from the coroner's officer. Under the cover of the noise, Mallett took the opportunity to whisper a few words to the coroner, who nodded in assent, and then returned to the witness.

"I have no more questions to ask you," he said.

Mr. Du Pine, looking profoundly relieved, took his uneasy presence from the box, and Jackie Roach succeeded him. He stumped forward in high feather at his own importance and grinned cheerfully at the coroner and at the jury. In honour of the occasion he had decorated his shabby coat with three tarnished war medals.

"Are you a newspaper seller?" asked the coroner.

"That's right, sir."

"I want you to take your mind back to last Friday evening. Where were you?"

"Corner of Upper Daylesford Street and the Gardens, sir."

"Carrying on your occupation there?"

"I beg your pardon?"

"Selling newspapers?"

"That's right, sir."

"Did you see anybody pass you while you were there?"

"Quite a number of people, sir."

"Anybody in particular—anyone you know?"

"I knows most of the people in the Gardens, sir."

The coroner tried another tack. "Do you know by sight the person who lived at No. 27?" he asked.

"Oh, Mr. James—yes, sir."

"You knew his name, then?"

"Yes, sir. Mr. Crabtree, what was doing for him, told me his name."

"You mean this Crabtree was his servant?"

"That's right, sir. He did for him."

"Did you see Mr. James that evening?"

"Yes, sir. He come past me on the opposite side of the road to where I was standing—him and another gentleman."

"About what time was that?"

"Round about half-past six, sir, more or less. I couldn't say for certain."

"Which way did they go?"

"Down the Gardens, sir, and into No. 27."

"They both went into the house? You are sure of that?"

"Yes, sir. I noticed that particular, because it was the first time ever I'd seen anyone go into that house since Mr. James come there, except Mr. Crabtree and Mr. James himself."

"Could you see who was with him?"

"No, sir, I couldn't. Mr. James was between him and me, and it was a bit darkish their side of the street."

"It was raining, was it not?"

"Just starting to drizzle, sir. Later on it came on to rain proper hard."

"But you are sure it was Mr. James?"

"Oh, yes, sir. I knows *him* all right. I've seen him, mornings and evenings, often."

"And did you see these two again later on?"

"Mr. James I did, sir, not the other one."

"Where was that?"

"Just outside of No. 27, sir. It had come on to rain, then, hard, and I was just going off down the Gardens to the public in Lower Daylesford Street. I heard the door bang and I looks round and see Mr. James going up the Gardens the way he'd come, walking fast."

"He was quite close to you, then?"

"Just the width of the street away, sir, that's all."

"Had he anything with him?"

"Just a bag in his hand, sir, same as he always carried. I don't know as I ever see'd him without it."

"Was he carrying it when you saw him first?"

"Oh, yes, sir, I'm sure he was."

"And what time was it when you saw him the second time?"

Roach paused a moment, and passed the back of his hand across his apology for a nose as an aid to memory. Then his face brightened and he said: "It was near on half-past seven when I got to the public, sir, and that's just five minutes from where I stands at the top of the Gardens."

63

"About twenty-five minutes past seven, then?"

"Just about, sir."

The coroner shuffled his papers, and glanced at Mallett. Mallett pursed his lips and nodded.

"Thank you," he said to Roach.

"Thank *you*, sir, and good morning," answered the newspaper seller cheerfully and stumped away.

"That is as far as we shall be able to go today, members of the jury," announced the coroner. "You will be informed if your presence is required again."

He rose and without further ceremony left the court. The crowd trickled slowly out, feeling elated that they had been present at an important function, but with the vague sense of disappointment that an anti-climax produces. As the last of them left the building, a plain clothes detective pushed his way in and came up to the inspector. "The man Crabtree has been found, sir," he said. "He is at the Yard now. I left instructions that no statement should be taken from him until you came."

"Quite right," answered Mallett. His thoughts for a moment turned longingly towards his lunch. But he suppressed the temptation. "I'll come at once," he said firmly.

10

The Trail of Mr. James

Wednesday, November 18th

On his arrival at Scotland Yard, Mallett went at once to his room. He was met there by a young officer, recently promoted, who had been assigned to him for assistance in the case, Detective-Sergeant Frant. He was a spare little man, full of dash, and supremely confident in his own abilities.

"Before you see this man, sir," he said, "there are one or two points I have cleared up for you."

"Very good of you," murmured Mallett.

"I have made enquiries from the railway officials," Frant went on. "I have ascertained that a man answering to the description of James travelled by the Newhaven boat-train on Friday night. He went first-class, and dined on the train. The Pullman attendant remembers him quite clearly, because he gave a lot of trouble and tipped him particularly well. I have put through an enquiry to Paris, but the answer isn't to hand yet."

"What about the passport officials?" asked Mallett.

"He had a passport, apparently. They have no recollection of him."

"They wouldn't. Well, have you been to the bank?"

"Yes. It appears that on Friday morning James called and took away his pass-book and a sealed packet which he had deposited with them. He also drew out all the money to his credit in one pound notes. I have seen the account. He paid in two hundred pounds in notes on the 16th October, the same day he took the house in Daylesford Gardens. The only payment out was the cheque to the house-agents. All they could give me at the bank were his two specimen signatures. Here they are."

He handed them over to the inspector, and added: "I have got the experts on to them, and they say they are obviously disguised—probably left-handed."

"You surprise me," said Mallett gravely. "Is that all?"

"So far as James is concerned—yes. But you ought to know—"

"The Southern Bank doesn't usually open an account without a reference of some kind," remarked Mallett.

The sergeant coloured. "The manager didn't mention anything of the sort to me," he answered.

"In other words, you forgot to ask him. That's not good enough, Frant. If you're going to succeed in this job, you must learn to be thorough. Get back to the bank, and tell the manager to turn up his records. There must be a letter of recommendation or something. What are you waiting for?"

Somewhat crestfallen, the sergeant said: "I thought I ought to mention, sir, a report has just come in that Fanshawe arrived in London from France this morning. He went to his sister's flat at 2b Daylesford Court Mansions."

Mallett made no reply for a moment. Then he said reflectively: "Were you at Fanshawe's trial, by any chance?"

"No—but I heard all about it, of course."

"I was. He was a curious chap. A thoroughbred gentleman, you'd have said, to look at him, and as cool as a cucumber. When he was found guilty and he was asked whether he had anything to say before sentence, he simply stuck his chin in the air and said: 'My lord, I only desire to state that if when I come out of prison Mr. Ballantine is still unhanged, I shall be happy to rectify the omission.' I can hear him now."

"And he did come out of prison," put in Frant eagerly, "and within a day Ballantine is dead."

"And we are looking for Mr. Colin James, who took a furnished house in Kensington while Fanshawe was in Maidstone Gaol," rejoined Mallett drily.

"Still, he had the opportunity to do it," put in Frant, "he may have been in touch with James. After all, two people were seen to go into the house."

"And only James came out, leaving a dead man behind. No, no, Frant, that cock won't fight. Still, it will be worth while to have a chat with Fanshawe some time soon. I suppose he is being kept under observation?"

"Yes."

"Good. And in the meantime we shall have an opportunity of finding out just what was Ballantine's part in the Fanshawe Bank affair when we go through his papers."

"That reminds me of the other thing I was to tell you," said the sergeant. "The London and Imperial Estates and its associated companies all filed their voluntary petitions in winding-up this morning."

"I'm not surprised. That place was simply a glorified bucket-shop. I suppose there will be the usual crop of prosecutions—false prospectuses and so on?"

"I've been talking to Renshaw, who's in charge of that investigation," said Frant, "and I gather that there won't be many directors left to prosecute, now that Ballantine is dead. Hartigan and Aliss, his two jackals, skipped the country a week ago, and Melbury, who has been ill in a nursing home for a month, only came up to business today to arrange about the petition and collapsed in the street and isn't expected to recover. That only leaves Du Pine, the secretary, and one director—Lord Henry Gaveston."

"Poor little guinea-pig," commented Mallett. "Well, thank goodness that isn't my pigeon. But tell Renshaw I want all Ballantine's private papers. This is murder, and it's got to come first. I'm not going to let any potty little Companies Acts affair stand in my way. Now off with you to the bank, and don't make a silly mistake like that again. And tell them to send up Crabtree. Lord, lord, when do I get my lunch?"

Mallett stilled the cravings of his stomach with a cigarette. He was not one of those whose brains are stimulated by privation, and he felt exhausted and dispirited. He knew he was only at the beginning of his investigations and that he would need every ounce of his strength to cope with them. And how could an all-too-human detective attend to the matters in hand properly when his thoughts would keep straying to a nicely grilled steak and tomato, with boiled apple pudding and cheese to follow?

These epicurean reflections were cut short by the arrival of Crabtree. It was heralded by much blasphemous language which echoed down the corridor, broken by the blander tones of an escorting police officer. When the door opened Mallett saw a truculent face, surmounting a short and tubby frame. It would have been difficult to guess at Crabtree's age. His grizzled hair and deeply lined cheeks were discounted by his muscular body and the vigour of his movements. "An old seaman," said Mallett to himself. "Certainly he swears like one."

Crabtree took the offensive at once.

"Now look 'ere," he demanded, "what are you perishing cops after, anyway? I've done my time, 'aven't I? Can't you leave a chap alone?"

"Sit down," said Mallett gently. "Where have you been all this time?"

"Been? In the lock-up, of course! Didn't they tell you?"

"What lock-up?" asked Mallett.

"Why, Spellsborough, of course. Drunk and assault. And then as soon as I gets 'ome, one of your blasted flats comes round and pulls me off 'ere. What's the game?"

Mallett became suddenly expansive and genial. He could, when necessary, adapt his manner to any company, and now, in his effort to put his visitor at his ease, he assumed an air of vulgar good-fellowship.

"Now look here, old man," he began confidentially, "we've got nothing on you. We thought you could help us in the hell of a big job we've got on here. That's all. I'm sorry about the Spellsborough business, but that's not my fault, is it? If I'd known you were there, I'd have had you out in no time. But I suppose you knew too much to give your proper name down there, eh? Here, sit down and have a fag."

Somewhat mollified, and deeply impressed by the inspector's quite unfounded suggestion that he could have released a prisoner from the cells at Spellsborough whenever he wished, Crabtree accepted the cigarette and sat down.

"Name?" he said. "Course I didn't give my name. Would you? Name of Crawford, I gave. And blowed if it wasn't the same name as the perishing chairman of the beaks! Gawd, that was a bad break, wasn't it?"

He guffawed at the recollection, and Mallett joined in with a discordant bray. Then he looked up at the officer who had brought in Crabtree and who was still waiting.

"I shan't want you any more," he said sharply. "And if this gentleman has to come here again, he's to be treated properly, see?"

The officer knew his Mallett. He clicked his heels together with exaggerated respect, boomed "Very good, sir," and departed well content with the part he had played in the little comedy.

Crabtree's respect for the inspector began to grow. It increased still further when this Olympian man, after so grand a display of authority, began immediately to discuss a subject next his heart.

"So you were at Spellsborough races?" he began. "Were you on Fidgety Lass for the Cup?"

"You bet your life I was," said Crabtree, now completely at his ease. "I'd got the straight tip from the stable on the Thursday, so down I went on Friday morning with every blinking bob I had. I didn't try a thing till the big race come along. Then I punted the lot on Fidgety Lass—I got eights about her, too. Lord, guv'nor, but she didn't 'alf give me the fidgets afore it was over! First time round she pecked at the water, and I thought she was down. She was near a length behind at the last fence, but in the run in 'er jock just showed 'er the whip, and she sailed 'ome. Coo, I cheered, I can tell you!"

"And what happened then?" asked Mallett with a grin.

"Blowed if I can tell you, guv'nor. Next thing I knew I was in the cells with a splitting 'ead and a mouth like the bottom of a parrot's cage. I 'eard all about it Monday morning, though. They didn't 'alf tell the tale. Five days the blighters gave me, without the option. I 'adn't no option, anyway. I was cleaned out."

"When did they let you out?"

"Tuesday morning, sir."

"You've taken your time getting home, then."

Crabtree swore at the recollection, and then described with picturesque violence his attempt to get a lift back to London.

"I sold the tin can for the price of a bite of food, sir," he concluded, "and footed it every step of the way back. I slept under a hedge on Tuesday night."

Mallett stroked his chin and pursed his lips. When he spoke again he was a good deal more like a police officer and less like a boon companion.

"At all events," he said, "you knew then that the police were anxious to interview you."

"I'd only read it in *The Daily Toiler*, sir," Crabtree protested. "You can't tell what to believe in that sort of paper, can you? Just Communist propaganda, ain't it?"

"And that a dead man has been found in Daylesford Gardens—that isn't Communist propaganda, you know."

"It wasn't there when I left, sir," said Crabtree in some agitation, "straight it wasn't."

"What time did you leave?" asked the inspector.

"Friday morning, sir, about 'alf-past nine. As soon as 'e'd finished breakfast, Mr. James calls for me and says, I shan't want you any more, Crabtree, 'e says, and 'e gives me my money and a quid extra to remember 'im by, and as soon as I'd cleared up the breakfast things off I went."

"Did Mr. James tell you he was going abroad?"

"Course 'e did, sir. 'E sent me round to Brook's the travel people in Daylesford Square, to get 'is ticket for 'im."

Mallett opened his blue eyes wide.

"Did he, indeed?" he said. "Where was the ticket for?"

"Paris, sir. First class, by the New'aven boat. And 'e told me to ask Brook's to book 'im a room in a 'otel, too."

"You don't remember the name of the hotel, I suppose?"

"No, sir. It was one of these foreign names. Wait a bit, though, 'e made me write it down before I went to Brook's. I may 'ave it on me still."

He fumbled in his pocket, and finally pulled out a crumpled piece of paper. This he unfolded and handed to Mallett. On it in rough capitals were the words: "Hotel Du Plessis, Avenue Magenta, Paris."

Mallett regarded it, frowning. "This is your handwriting, I suppose?" he said.

"Yes, sir. Mr. James spelt it out to me, same as you see it there. Come to think of it, I never saw 'im write anything, 'isself."

"And when was it you went to Brook's for the tickets?"

"That would be the Tuesday, sir, before 'e went."

Mallett spoke into the house telephone at his elbow.

"I want an enquiry put through to Paris at once," he said. "Ask them to be good enough to find out if anyone answering to the description of James arrived at the Hotel Du Plessis on Saturday morning." He added the address.

"Now tell me anything you can about Mr. James," he said to Crabtree.

What Crabtree could tell proved disappointingly little. It may best be summarized in the words of the notes which Mallett set down after the interview.

"Crabtree's description of James," wrote Mallett, "is vague, but agrees substantially with Harper's. He seems to have seen remarkably little of his employer. His duties were to keep the rooms clean and to prepare breakfast, the only meal James ever had there. He wasn't a particular man, Crabtree says, and couldn't bear women about the house. Refused the suggestion that a charwoman should come in to clear it up. C. is an old seaman and could turn his hand to what was necessary. The usual routine was for him to arrive at seven-thirty in the morning and heat the shaving water, which he would leave outside the bedroom door. James always kept his door locked. C. has never been inside it till James was up and dressed."

Mallett paused in his writing at this point and underlined the last two sentences heavily. He continued:

"James breakfasted at eight-thirty, and would leave the house between nine and half-past. He always carried a small bag or suitcase with him. (Compare Roach's statement.) C. would finish his work in the morning and not see him again till next day. Sometimes James would say he would not be home that night, and C. would find the bedroom empty in the morning. He is vague as to how often this happened, but thinks it may have been two or three times a week. The one thing that sticks in his mind is that it was a soft job. James never left any personal belongings lying about. Never had any visitors, so far as he knows. C. was unable to recognize a photograph of Ballantine when shown to him."

Here the document ended, but it was not the end of the interview. Something else passed between the inspector and Crabtree, which did not appear on the note, but which remained clearly etched on Mallett's retentive memory.

When Crabtree had finished his account, given with a compelling air of sincerity, Mallett said:

"There are just two more points I should like to know. Where did you stay at Spellsborough on Friday night?"

Crabtree shook his head, and a look of distrust came into his eyes.

"I can't tell yer that," he said. "There's a widder down there, see? And I don't want my old woman up 'ere to 'ear of it."

"You understand," persisted Mallett, "that it may be important for you to be able to say where you were on Friday night?"

Crabtree became sullen. "I won't do it, and that's that," he muttered.

Mallett did not press the point.

"The only other question is: how did you get this job with Mr. James?"

Crabtree answered this readily enough, though it was clear that his friendliness had vanished.

"Mr. 'Arper asked me if I wanted it, and I took it."

"That's the Mr. Harper in Inglewood, Browne's?"

"Just so."

"How did you know him?"

"Know 'im?" repeated Crabtree. "Of course I knew 'im. Didn't I teach 'im 'ow to 'andle a dinghy when 'is father was alive? Afore 'e lost all his money?"

Mallett drew a bow at a venture.

"Didn't he lose his money in a bank smash?" he asked.

"That's right—Fanshawe's Bank. Everything went then, 'ouse and 'orses—even the yacht. That was a fair tragedy, guv'nor," he went on, his eyes glazing with memories. "The prettiest little racing schooner you ever saw. She was bought by a gent up on the Clyde, and he's ruined 'er. Cut down 'er masts, raised 'er bulwarks—she's nothing but a regular old family barge now. It's enough to make a man cry. . . ."

"Have you ever heard young Mr. Harper mention Ballantine's name?" asked Mallett suddenly.

Crabtree, his head still full of dreams, came back to the present with a start.

"That—!" he exclaimed, "I should think I—"

He checked himself abruptly, and then with a puerile attempt at deception went on:

"What name did you say, sir? Ballantine? I'm sure I've never 'eard 'im mention that name in me life!"

He repeated with emphasis: "No, sir! Not Mr. 'Arper! Never!"

II

Mallett Feels Better

Wednesday, November 18th

The long delayed meal, and the pint of bitter that went with it, did Mallett good. It was fortunate, he reflected, as he puffed at his cigarette, that he was gifted with a good digestion. No detective, in his experience, could do his work satisfactorily unless he were on good terms with his stomach. Men are most proud of the qualities for which they have to thank nature rather than their own efforts, and Mallett's self-satisfaction remained with him as he took a brief post-prandial stroll in St. James's Park. It was, for London, an ideal November day. Over the leafless trees the sky was a clear pale blue, and there was a nip in the air that was invigorating without being chilly. Mallett paced the walks, breathing deep gulps of the wintry air, exulting in his own well-being. But when one is faced with a question of paramount importance, it will intrude itself everywhere, and any subject, however far removed from it, will, by some trick of the brain, present itself as in some way connected with the overmastering preoccupation. So it was with the inspector now. He stopped in mid-stride, swung on his heel and stared absently across the lake.

"Digestion, now!" he murmured to the unheeding pelicans. "What was it Harper said? A fattish man with a lean face, as though he had a bad digestion? Something like that. But Crabtree said he wasn't particular. Crabtree's cooking was pretty rough and ready, I should think, and he seems to have eaten his breakfasts all right. Odd!"

He remained irresolute for a few moments. Then, throwing the butt end of his cigarette at a fat pigeon near his feet, he muttered: "Well, it's a long shot, but it might be worth trying," and walked out of the park to St. James's Underground Station.

Mr. Benjamin Browne, sole partner of Inglewood, Browne and Company, was decidedly annoyed that afternoon when Lewis abruptly entered his room and told him that Inspector Mallett wished to see him at once. His annoyance was not due to the fact that the visit interrupted any important work, for he was doing none. He was being disturbed in something far more intimate and important than any work in the little nap which he was accustomed to take after lunch and to prolong, if possible, till tea-time. He objected still more to being caught in an undignified moment by Lewis, who had chosen to march in unannounced, to find his employer snoring in an arm-chair. Most of all, he objected to the grin of triumph on the young man's face, as he murmured hypocritically: "Sorry to disturb you, sir." In that instant, Lewis's fate was sealed. He was an indispensable employee, he knew, but there should be no partnership for him in Inglewood, Browne & Co.

Thus roughly awakened, Mr. Browne struggled to his feet.

"Ask him to wait a moment," he said.

"He says he hasn't long to spare," replied Lewis, rejoicing in his principal's discomfiture. "He would like to see you at once."

"Tell him to wait," repeated Browne. "I can't see him like this, can I?"

He clawed on the greasy tail-coat which he had taken off before his slumbers, ran to a mirror in the corner of the room, resettled his dishevelled black tie, dabbed with a hairbrush at his almost entirely bald head, stroked into submission his weeping black moustache, and finally settled down behind his desk.

"Now," he said to Lewis, pulling some documents before him, "ask him to come in."

Mallett took in the office at a glance—the dusty files, the empty letter-tray, the crumpled arm-chair. "Not much business here," he thought.

"Good afternoon," said Browne ponderously, stifling a yawn. "It's this Daylesford Gardens business, I suppose? Can we assist you in any way?"

"I hope so," said Mallett. "I am sorry to have to disturb you—"

"Not at all, not at all," Browne assured him. "To tell you the truth, we were rather busy today"—he waved his hand in a manner that he hoped would be impressive—"but we are always ready to assist the cause of justice, I'm sure."

"As a matter of fact," said the inspector, "I came here in the hope of seeing Mr. Harper. But I'm told he is out."

Browne shook his head sadly.

"I'm afraid that young man takes his duties very lightly, Inspector," he said. "I had to give him leave to go to the inquest this morning, of course, and Mr. Lewis too—very inconvenient to me, we have only a small staff here, as you see, but naturally the claims of the law must be met and he has not returned. Simply absented himself. It's very galling, Inspector. That is the word—galling." He breathed heavily and pulled at the long points of his moustache.

"Tell me about Mr. Harper," said Mallett confidentially. "Has he been with you long?"

"Four or five years," answered Browne. "And between you and me, sir, he has been a most unsatisfactory young man. Most unsatisfactory. It was the late Mr. Inglewood who engaged him, out of friendship for his father, I understood. And from respect to Mr. Inglewood's memory, more than anything else, I kept him on. He was a fine gentleman, Mr. Inglewood," went on the house agent, shaking his bald head dolefully. "He had a wonderful way with the better-class clients, if you follow me. It was a great loss to the firm when he was taken."

He stared at his desk, contemplating the ghosts of vanished better-class clients, till Mallett recalled him to his surroundings with: "And Mr. Harper?"

"Ah, Mr. Harper, just so. His father was ruined, I understand, in that big bank failure some years ago—you would know the name, Inspector—"

"Fanshawe?" put in Mallett.

"Fanshawe—yes. And what made matters worse, Mr. Inglewood told me, Fanshawe was an old friend of the late Mr. Harper. And he ruined him, simply ruined him."

"That was very hard luck," said the inspector.

"Very. Oh, I was sorry for the young man, I assure you. That is why I kept him on here. Besides, there was always the chance that he might bring some of his better-class friends here as clients. But he didn't. And hard luck doesn't excuse his being so shockingly careless in his work as he's been. This Daylesford Gardens matter, for instance. That has been a bad business for us, Inspector. Why, there's three pounds two and sixpence owing to Miss Penrose for dilapidations, and how we're going to collect it from the tenant now, I don't know."

"But you were telling me about Mr. Harper," Mallett interrupted.

"Exactly. Now, for instance, I had your Sergeant Frant round here yesterday asking to see the lease which Mr. James signed. Could Mr. Harper find it? He could not. He thought he'd put it somewhere, he said, but we searched high and low and it wasn't to be found. Now I call that sort of thing galling, Inspector."

"Now we are on that subject," said Mallett, "have you any letters or documents signed by Mr. James at all?"

"Not one," said Browne. "Except for the lease, there was only the cheque for the rent, and Mr. Harper took that himself and paid it in."

"But he returned the keys by post, didn't he? Wasn't there a letter with them?"

"I'll ask Mr. Lewis," said Browne.

Lewis was summoned from the outer office and the same question put to him.

"There was a letter with the keys," he answered. "I remember Harper told me so."

"Then wasn't it filed in the usual way?" asked Browne.

"It ought to have been, of course," said Lewis, evidently pleased to be able to score off his fellow employee, "But it wasn't. I looked for it myself, and when I asked Harper, he said he thought it didn't matter, and he'd thrown it away."

Mr. Browne threw up his hands in despair.

"There you are, you see!" he exclaimed. "That's him all over! What can you do with a man like that? I believe he's in love, Inspector, engaged or something, but it doesn't excuse that sort of thing."

"I quite agree with you," said Mallett. "Good afternoon, Mr. Browne, and let me know if Mr. Harper comes in later."

Mallett, on his journey back to Scotland Yard, had food for thought. It was extraordinary how successfully

James had succeeded in hiding his traces. Outwardly, nothing would have been more open, ostentatious even, than his actions. To open an account at a bank, to engage a furnished house and a servant, to take a ticket to Paris through an agency here was a series of actions which should have left behind a trail of clues to his identity—to his handwriting at least, from which his identity could have been established. Instead, there was nothing, or next to nothing, unless Frant's second visit to the bank should prove more fruitful than his first. It was impossible even to lay hands on anybody who had ever spoken to him, except Crabtree and Harper. He frowned. Why should Harper have been so shockingly careless about the tenancy agreement and the letter? He would not willingly believe that this well-bred, good-looking young man could have had a hand in a callous crime, but if it were only coincidence, it was a very unfortunate one that the one person who had the opportunity of supplying valuable evidence should, knowingly or not, have been the means of destroying it.

Well, thought Mallett, James was in Paris, it seemed certain. Probably the French police would manage to find him. But they had little information to work on, not even a proper description. Nobody seemed to have noticed anything outstanding about him except his beard, and that could be shaved off easily enough. Somewhere in London there must be people who could tell more about him. Somewhere there must be the evidence which would link him with Ballantine, which would explain how Ballantine came to go to his death in that quiet little backwater in Kensington. All the indications were to the effect that here was a carefully prepared crime. It could not have been contrived without leaving some traces of its machinery. And he, Mallett, if anybody, was the man to find them. He gave his moustache an upward twist and looked so fierce that the lady sitting opposite in the train, catching sight of him over her magazine, started nervously.

On his desk at Scotland Yard he found a telegram from the Sûreté at Paris. Translated it ran: "James traced to Hotel Du Plessis. Search continues. Letter follows."

"I wish these French weren't so damned economical," said Mallett. "Now we shall have to wait till tomorrow for the details."

Sergeant Frant entered, in a state of some excitement.

"I've got what you want, sir," he said.

"Well?"

Frant laid a letter before him. It was typewritten on the notepaper of the London and Imperial Estates Company, Ltd. It was addressed to the Branch Manager of the Southern Bank, and ran as follows:

13th October, 19—

Dear Sir,

   This is to introduce Mr. Colin James, a gentleman well known to us. We are confident that you will extend to him all facilities in your power.

Yours faithfully,

LONDON & IMPERIAL ESTATES LTD.
Henry Gaveston,
Director.

"Gaveston!" exclaimed Mallett. "Of all people! Lord Henry Gaveston!"

"Well, even lords have some queer friends now and again," remarked Frant. "But it's what we want, isn't it? Here's the link between James and Ballantine."

"Yes, and the very last we expected," answered the inspector. "Have you got into touch with him?"

"His lordship is out of town, according to his valet," said Frant. "He wouldn't or couldn't give the address."

"I don't think that need trouble us," Mallett replied. "A man like Lord Henry won't go into hiding for long. We've got to have a chat with him, and the sooner the better!"

Feeling much relieved, he hummed a little tune as he sat down at his desk. Things were beginning to move at last!

12

Inquest on a Business

Thursday, November 19th

The letter from Paris was in Mallett's hands next morning. He read it through aloud, translating literally as he went, for the benefit of Frant. The writer acknowledged the receipt of the enquiries of his respected colleague and in reply hastened to submit for his consideration and information the matters following, namely: that immediately upon receipt of the advice and enquiries aforesaid he, the undersigned, had personally caused an investigation to be made at the Hotel Du Plessis, Ave. Magenta, Paris, 9e., and submitted to an interrogation strict and detailed the manager and staff of the hotel; that from such interrogation and examination of the relevant correspondence it was made manifest that the suspect James had veritably descended at the said hotel at 5:50 hours or thereabouts on Saturday and there lodged in a room previously reserved for him by the Agence Brook (room No. 323, on the third floor, with private bathroom, at a tariff of francs 65). The undersigned pointed out that such behaviour on the part of the suspect James was in conformity with his having fulfilled his expressed intention of making the crossing by the route Newhaven-Dieppe, precisely as the distinguished information of his colleague had suggested. Unhappily, by an oversight possibly unintentional but none the less criminal, one had not fulfilled the requisite formalities of the law and the said James had ascended to his room without signing the form provided for the surveillance of foreign voyagers in France. For this contravention one would rigorously pursue the hotel proprietors before the Correctional Tribunal of the Department of the Seine.

"Very right and proper," grunted Mallett, "but that won't help us to a sight of James's handwriting." He resumed his reading.

One had served breakfast to the aforesaid individual at 10:30 hours in his room, it appeared, whereafter he had immediately descended to the street and after regulating his account departed on foot carrying his suitcase. The undersigned had given formal instruction for his pursuit and detention, but so far one had found nobody of his description. The staff of the hotel declared him to be to all indications a serious individual—

"What does that mean?" asked Frant.

"Simply that he didn't look like a crook," said Mallett.

—and of appearance and accent markedly Britannic. They pretended to be able to recognize him even without his beard, of which, without doubt, the suspect would seek without delay to disembarrass himself. Considering the measures in force in France for the control of strangers, it was not probable that the assassin would long escape the hands of Justice, unless indeed he had already returned to his own country.

"That sounds rather a doubtful compliment to us," was the inspector's comment.

The undersigned awaited with lively anticipation further particulars of the individual aforesaid and requested his collaborator to accept the expression of his most distinguished sentiments.

"And that's all," said Mallett, laying down the flimsy typed sheets. "Except for the signature, and that's completely illegible anyway."

"But it's a lot, isn't it?" put in Frant eagerly. "It lets us out, anyway."

"It does not let us out," Mallett answered emphatically. "In the first place, we've got to establish that James is the murderer. It looks like it, I agree, but we haven't proved it yet. In the second place, we must find out who he is, and what is his connection with Ballantine. Luckily that letter to the bank gives us a pretty good line on that."

"When we find Lord Henry Gaveston," objected Frant.

"You ought to read *The Times* more carefully," replied the inspector. "Especially the social columns. Look here."

He indicated a paragraph with his finger, and Frant, following his direction, read:

"Arrivals at the Riviera Hotel, Brighton, include Sir John and Lady Bulpit, the Bishop of Foxbury and Mrs. Escott, and Lord Henry Gaveston."

"Not much concealment there," said Frant.

"No. Which makes me think . . . However, it's no use building theories until we get the facts. Where was I? Oh, yes. In the third place, we don't know for certain whether James stopped in France or whether he doubled home again. This trip to Paris may have been simply to throw us off the scent, and I dare say he would find his markedly Britannic accent rather a handicap if he wanted to go into hiding on the Continent. In any case there's a lot of work to be done at this end. If we can find out how Ballantine came to go to Daylesford Gardens, we shall have done something. We shall have to go pretty deep into his private life—find out where he'd been living and who with—you remember his wife's evidence—who had a motive for killing him, and so on. Meanwhile a trip to Brighton seems indicated."

The telephone bell rang. Mallett took off the receiver and found himself speaking to Mr. Benjamin Browne.

"It's about that young man, Harper," said Mr. Browne's voice. "You asked me yesterday, Inspector, if you remember—"

"Yes, yes," said Mallett. "Of course I remember. What about him?"

"He has just come in here," went on Mr. Browne in deliberate tones.

"Well, ask him to be good enough to come up to Scotland Yard at once."

"But he isn't here now," said Mr. Browne peevishly. "He just looked in—just poked his head into my room, Inspector, and said he was resigning his position. And then he walked out—simply walked out without any further notice. After all I had done for him, too! It's really very—"

"Very galling, no doubt," agreed Mallett. "Did you tell him I wanted to see him?"

"I didn't have the chance. I was so flabbergasted by his behaviour. And he didn't tell me where he was going or what he was going to do. He was so cool about it, it quite took my breath away. It is, as you say, most ga—"

Mallett rang off.

The inspector's trip to Brighton was postponed to a later hour than he had intended. The afternoon was spent in close conference with Renshaw, the officer in charge of the investigation of the affairs of the London and Imperial Estates Company and its associated concerns.

Renshaw was supported by a couple of dour accountants and an enormous sheaf of documents, the first fruits of his enquiries into the ramifications of what the newspapers were already openly calling "the great Ballantine swindle". Mallett was fond of representing himself as a simple man—which he was not—and as having a horror for complicated figures—which he had. But under the skillful guidance of the experts he found himself being led, fascinated, through endless labyrinths of crooked finance. The details were complicated, as they must always be where every action taken has to be accompanied by half a dozen others whose sole intent is to hide the real meaning of the transaction; but the general effect of the story revealed was plain enough. Ballantine had been practising, with extreme cleverness and several variations of his own devising, a very familiar form of swindle. With a number of companies to play off one against the others, and the means and the ability to rig the market in the shares of any or all of them, he had pursued the old game of robbing Peter to pay Paul and borrowing from Paul when Peter's balance sheet had to be presented. That was how Mallett, with his usual bluntness of phrase, put the position, and the accountants, though shocked at his unscientific way of expressing it, agreed that roughly—very roughly—that might be said to be the method.

"Only, of course," Renshaw remarked, "it wasn't a case of Peter and Paul only, but a whole lot more. In fact, in the City, Ballantine's companies were known as the Twelve Apostles. One or two of them never seem to have functioned at all. I fancy he just had them registered to make up the round dozen."

"And all of them, I suppose, with their offices at the same address?" asked the inspector.

"Yes; though oddly enough among his private papers we found a reference to another one—the Anglo-Dutch

Rubber and General Trading Syndicate—with an address in Bramston's Inn, off Fetter Lane. Ballantine paid the rent for the offices monthly, but it never seems to have done any business, and when I went there the place was completely empty and had been for some time, apparently."

Mallett nodded, mechanically taking a note of the address. Once he had established the general crookedness of the late financier, the details of his devices did not interest him greatly. As to the eventual aim of all his dealings, that became clear enough as the enquiry proceeded. It was simply to divert money through one channel or another from the pockets of the investing public into those of Ballantine, and equally clearly it had been remarkably successful. Then quite suddenly, during the last few days of his life, things had gone against him. He had been unexpectedly attacked by a leading financial newspaper, and the shareholders in his principal concern, with the annual general meeting on the horizon, had lost confidence. The market quotations had fallen catastrophically, and on the very day of his death his enemies were in full cry.

"The game was up, and he knew it," said Renshaw. "Now if he had committed suicide one could have understood it."

"He would certainly have saved us a lot of trouble if he had," remarked Mallett. "Instead of which, he let someone else do the job, and left us with the business of avenging his worthless self. But I don't think he was the man to take his own life. Why didn't he run for it, like Aliss and Hartigan?"

"So far as we can make out, that's just what he did."

"Yes—as far as Daylesford Gardens."

"I think he meant to go farther than that," answered Renshaw.

He went on to explain the result of his researches into Ballantine's conduct on his last day of business. For some time previously he had been apparently unusually erratic in his behaviour, arriving late and leaving early, but on this day he had been almost continuously in his private room at the office. What he did there could only be surmised from the state of his belongings afterwards, but it seemed clear that he had spent a good deal of time in destroying papers. His private safe was almost empty, and Mallett was disappointed to learn that nothing connecting him with Fanshawe had survived. He had withdrawn from his private banking account the sum standing to his credit, and his passport was missing from the drawer where it was usually kept.

"Altogether," Renshaw concluded, "it seems pretty clear that he had a longer journey in mind than to Kensington."

"It also seems pretty clear," rejoined Mallett, "that he must have had a good deal of money on him when he was killed. How much, do you think?"

Renshaw shook his head.

"That we shall never know exactly, I am afraid," he answered. "There was only a hundred pounds or so in cash in his private account when it was closed, but there had been some very big sums passing through it during the last few months. Where it all went to, it is difficult to say. If, as I guess, he was afraid to face the shareholders at the meeting, and meant to run away, no doubt he had put away a little nest-egg somewhere—abroad, probably. Of the actual payments we can trace, many were to women."

"Including his wife?" asked Mallett, remembering Mrs. Ballantine's evidence at the inquest.

"No. She had been clever or lucky enough to get a handsome settlement out of him some time ago. So far as she was concerned, it was the other way about. From what we can gather, it seems that just before he went he was trying to get her to consent to raise money on the settlement, but she refused."

"Of course—she would. Then these other women are—"

"All sorts. He seems to have been generous in an odd sort of way, and kept up quite big allowances to discarded mistresses. Then he's been supporting the Italian dancer, Fonticelli—but that affair came to an end some time ago. The largest payments recently were all to Mrs. Eales."

"I think I have heard of her," said Mallett. "Was she the reigning favourite?"

"Yes. Ballantine has been living with her, except when it suited him to turn up at Belgrave Square, quite regularly for over a year now. He set her up in rather a nice flat in Mount Street. It was quite an open affair. Everybody knew about it in the office."

Mallett was silent for a moment.

"Mount Street is a long way from Daylesford Gardens," he said at last. "All the same, I think I must put Mrs. Eales next on my list to be visited. As I see my problem, Renshaw, apart from yours, there are two lines to work on. One is to take James from where he first appears as a tenant of Miss Penrose's house, and trace him backwards until he meets Ballantine. The other is to work on Ballantine and trace him forwards, so to speak, until he meets James. Both are worth following up, and it seems to me that if anyone can help me to some knowledge of Ballantine's private life it will be Mrs. Eales."

"One other person could give you a good deal of information if he wanted to," said Renshaw.

"You mean Du Pine?" Mallett said at once.

Renshaw nodded. "He and the two missing directors were the only people who were privy to Ballantine's frauds," he added. "Du Pine was in it up to the neck. We've got quite enough to arrest him on now."

"I hope you'll do nothing of the sort," interposed the inspector. "A prisoner under arrest can't be questioned, and I think that Du Pine free will be more useful to me than under lock and key. We'll have him kept under observation, though."

"He practically begged me to arrest him this morning when we were at the office with him," said Renshaw. "Do you think he knows the Judges' Rules and feels he would be safer that way?"

"I dare say he knows a lot," replied Mallett, "but not so much as I shall know by this evening, I hope."

13

Mother and Son

Thursday, November 19th

Frank Harper was packing. The flimsy floors and walls of the little house echoed to the crash of drawers opening and shutting and to his loud shouts of annoyance as he pursued his elusive belongings up and down his untidy bedroom. Mrs. Harper heard him as she came in, her arms full of the fruits of an afternoon's arduous shopping. Characteristically, she dropped them all where she stood in the shabby passage that did duty for a hall, and ran upstairs at once to her son's room.

"Frank!" she exclaimed, pushing her untidy grey hair back from her eyes. "Whatever are you doing?"

"Packing," he answered briefly. "Haven't I got a clean evening shirt anywhere?"

"In the linen cupboard, dear. I'll get it for you. But why? Where are you off to?"

"To Lewes. And I haven't too much time to catch my train, either. Do get that shirt, Mother, there's a darling."

Mrs. Harper obediently trotted away, a puzzled frown

on her kindly, stupid face, and returned almost immediately.

"Here it is, dear," she said. "I had to darn the neck, but it really doesn't show when you've got it on."

"Thanks, Mother." He examined the darn disdainfully. "Oh well, I suppose it will have to do." He crammed the shirt on to the top of the overflowing suitcase. "Now I think that's everything."

"You've forgotten your sponge-bag, haven't you, darling?"

"Good lord, yes! Now how the devil am I to get that in?"

"Shall I do it for you?" Mrs. Harper was on her knees, coaxing recalcitrant objects into place with her toil-worn fingers. "But why to Lewes, dear?"

"I'm staying the night with the Jenkinsons. You know, I've told you about her—about them, I mean."

"Oh, yes, of course. I'm so silly nowadays, I forget people's names. I hope you enjoy yourself." Then she paused in her work and looked up at him. "But Frank, how is it that you're not at work?"

Frank laughed.

"I've left that place," he said. "For good."

"Left it? Oh Frank, you don't mean that Mr. Browne has—"

"Given me the sack? No. Though, bless his innocent little heart, he's had cause enough to. No, Mother, I have resigned. Place didn't suit, as the servants say. Behold in your son a gentleman of leisure."

"Left—left Inglewood, Browne's? I don't understand. Of course, I'm glad, if you didn't like the place. And I shall love to have you at home. Only—only I'm afraid you'll find it very dull here with nothing to do. And—and what about your pocket money? You've always been able to keep yourself in clothes and things out of what you've earned. I can help you a little perhaps, but it's not much. And, you know, my money is only an annuity. If anything should happen to me—"

She bent her head over the suitcase to hide her confusion.

"There, Mother, that's splendid. I can shut it myself. Let me give you an arm to help you up. Oops!"

He pulled her to her feet, and bending down, kissed her with unexpected tenderness.

"You're not to worry about me," he said. "I'm not going to come back here and hang about the house all day. Quite the contrary. Once more, in the language of the servants' hall, I've left to better myself."

"You've got another post, then? A better one? What is it? Another house agent?"

Frank smiled happily.

"No, not a house agent," he said. "I'm going away, Mother, a long way away—that is, if Susan is still of the same mind as she was last Sunday. And you, relieved of the burden of your worthless child, are going to live at that cottage in Berks or Bucks or wherever it is you've always wanted to go, until such time as I return, rich with all the spoils of Africa—"

"Africa! Frank, you're talking nonsense!"

"I am not! Africa I said, and to Africa I mean to go."

"But how are you going to get to Africa?" persisted the perplexed old lady.

"Oh, by train and boat, I expect. That is the usual way, isn't it? Unless I fly. Which reminds me, unless I do fly, now, I'm not going to get to Victoria in time."

He fastened the suitcase with an effort.

"Good-bye, Mother, and don't forget about the cottage. I mean it."

He laughed down at her bewilderment, and kissed her

again. "Back tomorrow, I expect," he said. "I shall have a lot to do.

> "*For there are great things to be done,*
> *And fine things to be seen,*
> *Before we go to Paradise——*"

"Frank!" She called him back as he was in the doorway, the suitcase swinging in his hand.

"Yes, what is it?"

"I had forgotten to tell you. Someone was asking about you today."

"About me? Who?"

"A policemen."

"A policeman?"

The suitcase fell from his hand to the floor with a crash. The shock sprung the catch and the lid flew open. The carefully packed contents strewed the floor.

"Damned clumsy of me," muttered Frank. "No, don't you bother, Mother, I'll do it."

He crammed the things back into place and forced down the lid with a savage jerk. Then he straightened himself, his face red with exertion.

"What did he want?"

"Who? Oh, the policeman. It was only the sergeant from the police station round the corner. Quite a nice man, I see him often. Nothing to worry about, dear."

"Who said there was anything to worry about?" asked her son defiantly.

Mrs. Harper took no notice of the interruption and went on:

"I think it was just this horrible inquest business he came about. He had been sent to verify your address and so on, he said. I told him all about us and he took particulars and seemed quite satisfied. That's all. I thought you would like to know."

"Oh, well, if that's all . . . Look here, Mother, if by any chance you have anybody—*anybody*, police or not—coming round here again while I'm away—not that I suppose you will, for a moment, but one never can tell—just keep what I told you under your hat, do you mind? About Africa, I mean, and Susan and all the rest of it. No point in having them poking into our affairs, is there?"

"No, of course not, darling. I don't know anything really myself, so I can't say anything, can I?"

He laughed. "That's the spirit, Mum. And mum's the word!"

He was gone. Mrs. Harper, with a sigh, began to tidy the chaos of her son's room. She did not in the least understand what Frank had told her. She did not believe all his grandiose talk about Africa and a cottage in the country. But then for years now she had lived in a dim twilight of existence, where the only reality was the ever-present necessity of making both ends meet, the only illumination the love and pride which she felt for her son. Dimly she was aware that there had been a time when life went easily and comfortably, when there was leisure to think and to enjoy, and when the prices of things in the shops were a matter of casual interest. It did not seem real now, any more than Frank's sudden optimism about the future seemed real. It only unsettled one to hope for impossibilities. But one thing at least was real—the fact that her moody, discontented son was for some reason happy and hopeful once more. And without understanding, she basked in the rays of his cheerfulness. After all, they had been ruined in the past for reasons which had always remained somewhat of a mystery to her. Why should they not regain their fortunes in an equally inexplicable way? And if for some cause it was the price of fortune to keep it a close secret—well, she reflected, one thing an old woman could do was to keep her own counsel.

She stopped in her work, her contentment suddenly clouded over. Frank had gone away with an odd pair of socks!

14

Lord Henry and Lord Bernard

Thursday, November 19th

An electric train carried Mallett smoothly Brighton-wards, together with a crowd of homing stockbrokers. The chatter of his neighbors in the carriage seemed to be equally divided between golf and the Ballantine affair—the latter being viewed exclusively from the financial standpoint. He was agreeably surprised to learn from their talk that each of them had, by superhuman foresight, succeeded in "getting out" of the Twelve Apostles at the very top of the market. He also learned several novel items of information—amongst others that the Commissioner of Police had "dropped a packet" on London Imperials and therefore was making no particular efforts to trace the financier's murderer. An elderly man in the corner was bold enough to hint his doubts of the accuracy of the last statement, but was instantly suppressed.

"Fact!" said the narrator, a stout young man with an aggressive voice. "Chap I knew had it direct from a pal of his who's in Scotland Yard."

This was too much for Mallett's gravity, and he hastily

took up an evening paper to hide his smiles. Here he found that although now three days old, the "Mystery of Daylesford Gardens" still retained enough vitality to keep itself in the headlines, though fresh sensations had crowded it off the front page. He read with interest of an entirely mythical "police dash" to Birmingham, from which important results were understood to have been obtained; and had just embarked on an article by the City Editor on the probable effects of the London and Imperial liquidation which puzzled his unmathematical brains a good deal more even than Renshaw's accountants had done, when a name uttered by the same loud-voiced man caught his ear and riveted his attention.

"Bernie Gaveston is on the train," he said. "I saw him get into the next carriage."

"Who?" asked someone.

"Bernie—*Lord* Bernard Gaveston. You know who I mean?"

"Oh! Yes, of course," was the answer. Then, respectfully: "Do you know him?"

"Rather! Matter of fact, he was staying at Gleneagles the same time as we were last year. I used to see him nearly every day."

"You never mentioned it before," said the elderly man from his corner.

"Well, of course, I didn't see much of him—not to speak to, I mean. He had his own crowd there with him. But I was always running into him, in the bar and so on. I thought he seemed a nice sort of chap. Funny thing is, I haven't set eyes on him since, and now here he is in the next carriage. Shows what a small place the world is, doesn't it?"

Mallett chuckled quietly behind his paper. The idea of this underbred little man claiming acquaintance with the famous Lord Bernard Gaveston amused him hugely. For Lord Bernard was, as every reader of the illustrated weeklies knew, a celebrity of the first order. It was difficult to know exactly why. He had never done anything particularly startling—never gone into Parliament or, like his unlucky brother, into the City. He had been content to remain an ornament to Society, and done it very well. He had written a couple of not very successful plays and composed some not very distinguished music. But his clothes were the despair and admiration of every young man who aspired to be well dressed, his appearance at a new restaurant or night-club was the guarantee of its success, his photograph was almost as familiar to the public as that of the most boomed débutante—in a word he was News, with a capital N, and there were very few young men of whom that could be said.

At the same time, the inspector was not a little annoyed at Lord Bernard's appearance on the train. Obviously it was connected in some way with Lord Henry's presence in Brighton. There was not the smallest reason to suppose that he had anything to do with his brother's business adventures, but the inspector had come down to interview one man, and he was not best pleased to find that he might have to do with two. So far as Lord Henry was concerned, he thought he knew fairly well what to expect. He was the stupid type of titled man, with a fair record of military service behind him, who would appeal to one such as Ballantine as likely to give a good appearance to a list of directors. Nobody would expect him to be concerned in his chairman's fraudulent schemes or even to have the brains to understand them, and the only mystery was how it came about that of all the people connected with Ballantine he alone appeared to provide the link between him and Colin James. That mystery it was Mallett's present business to clear up and if it came to a contest of wits he was fairly confident of the issue. But

Lord Bernard—he shrugged his broad shoulders—was a different matter. He was without doubt, in his own way, a clever man. Lord Henry had read the account of the inquest in the papers, no doubt, and sent for his brother to assist and advise him. Under the influence of that shrewd man of the world, would he refuse to give any information? And what would Mallett's remedy be if he did? He put down his paper and frowned out of the window at the darkened sky.

Whatever hopes the inspector may have had of reaching the Riviera Hotel before Lord Bernard and so of securing at least part of his interview without interference, were quickly disappointed. As he alighted on the station platform almost the first person he saw was Lord Bernard, being greeted by an obsequious chauffeur. Evidently Lord Henry was expecting his brother's arrival. Before Mallett's elderly taxi could clear the station, it was passed by a low open car of venomously speedy design, with Lord Bernard at the wheel, the chauffeur sitting beside him. "Not the sort of car I should have expected Lord Henry to own," said Mallett to himself. "I thought he was a steady-going sort of stupid."

The rear light of the car twinkled for a moment among the traffic ahead and was lost to view, and the inspector resigned himself to a comparatively slow journey to the hotel. The tall mauve lamps of Brighton front slid by in leisurely procession as the asthmatic vehicle chugged along. At last a violent grinding of brakes told him that he had arrived. Lord Bernard, he calculated, as he paid his fare, had about five minutes' start of him. Much harm could be done in five minutes. He cursed Renshaw for having been the unconscious cause of his delay. Had it not been for him, Lord Henry could have been interviewed, and he, Mallett, back in London, before Lord Bernard had even started. So absorbed was he in these reflections that he miscounted his change and only the driver's surprised "Thank *you*, sir!" revealed to him that he had grossly overtipped the man.

The mistake aggravated Mallett's sense of grievance with the world. Everything seemed to be going wrong with him. He did not grudge the driver an unearned shilling, but the fact that he, the most careful of men, should have made such a stupid blunder, annoyed him intensely. It was only by reminding himself that he might well be within a few moments of the most important discovery since he had begun his investigations, that he was able to regain his sense of proportion.

"Is Lord Henry Gaveston in the hotel?" Mallett asked the sleek and supercilious reception clerk.

"Yes, he is," admitted the functionary. His eyes travelled up and down the inspector's burly form and an expression of discomfort crept into his smooth features. "But I don't know whether he can see you. You are not from the Press, by any chance?"

"No. Scotland Yard," said Mallett bluntly.

The clerk's pained look was that of a prude in whose hearing an obscenity had been blurted out. He glanced involuntarily round the brilliantly lighted, over-decorated hall, at the monumental back of the gorgeous commissionaire outside, as though to say: "Not here! Not in the Riviera, of all places!" But he pulled himself together like a man, and with a fine show of sang-froid murmured: "In that case, I'll have him paged."

A small uniformed boy, uttering the high-pitched wail peculiar to his class, was duly sent out on his tour of the Smoking Room, Winter Garden, Drawing-Room and Ye Olde Tudor Lounge. Duly he returned, announcing with evident relish: "No reply, sir!" where-upon Mallett, turning on his heel, found himself look-ing directly into a small recess bounded by a cocktail bar. In front of the bar was a little table, and at the table, not ten yards away, sat Lord Henry and his brother.

Mallett indicated the bar with his finger. "Did you try in there?" he asked the page.

"Oh, no, sir!" came the instant reply. "The gentlemen in there, they never likes to be disturbed."

"Smart lad," said Mallett, too amused to be annoyed. "Perhaps you'll have a hotel of your own some day."

Leaving the page scarlet with pleasure at what he dim-ly apprehended to be a compliment, the inspector strode across the intervening space and bore down upon the two men.

There was a strong family resemblance between the two brothers. They each had the same rather promi-nent, well-cut nose, the same arched eyebrows over light grey eyes, the same delicately rounded chin. But while Lord Bernard's eyes were clear and vivacious, Lord Henry's were pale and watery. His raised eye-brows gave an impression of peevish surprise at what the world had to show him, in contrast to his brother's alert look of amused inquisitiveness. The elder of the two by a few years only, he was already beginning to go bald, and his face to sag before the onset of mid-dle age. Lord Bernard, on the other hand, with his thick brown hair and clear complexion, might have stood model for an advertisement of anybody's patent medicine.

As Mallett drew near, Lord Henry was setting down an empty tumbler with the melancholy air of a man who was conscious that the contents had done him little good. Lord Bernard was contemplating a cocktail in his hand

and appeared to be addressing it, rather than his brother, in low and soothing tones. Both looked up as the inspector approached.

"Lord Henry Gaveston?" said Mallett.

Lord Henry, characteristically, turned towards his brother for help. The latter appraised Mallett in a swift glance.

"You're a detective, I take it," he said.

Mallett nodded. Lord Bernard rose quickly, laid his hand lightly on his senior's shoulder and said:

"I suggest, old man, that another whiskey and soda would do you no harm at this moment."

Lord Henry said nothing, but dumbly relinquished the tumbler he was still clutching, and his brother bore it off to the bar.

Mallett was agreeably surprised that he should have been left alone with his man for a few moments even. He knew from experience the importance of a suspect's first reaction when confronted with a damning piece of evidence and he determined to lose no time. Without further preamble he drew from his pocket the letter to the bank, unfolded it, and handed it across the table.

"I want to ask you a few questions about this," he said.

Lord Henry, his hands shaking visibly, stared at the document for a moment. Then he fumbled in his pockets, produced an old-fashioned pair of pince-nez, and adjusted them with difficulty on his nose. With this assistance he slowly read the letter through, forming the words with his mouth as he went. Finally he said, in obviously genuine bewilderment:

"But I don't understand. What is all this about?"

"That is exactly what I have come to ask you," retorted Mallett in some irritation. In the background he could see Lord Bernard approaching, a brimming glass in his hand. "Is that your signature, or is it not?"

"Oh, certainly it's mine all right," returned Lord Henry dolefully. "No doubt about that. The office paper, too. But who is Mr. Colin James? Never heard of the feller in my life."

"Colin James", said Mallett impressively, "is suspected of the murder of Lionel Ballantine."

"Here's your drink, Harry," said Lord Bernard, depositing a whisky and soda on the table and dropping into a chair. "Ballantine's murder, eh? A nasty business. You don't know anything about it, do you, old man?" He turned to Mallett. "You know, I thought you had come to bother Harry about this London and Imperial Estates business," he confided.

"I am enquiring into the death of Lionel Ballantine," said the inspector stolidly, "and I am here to ask Lord Henry how he came to sign a letter recommending Mr. Colin James—"

"James!" put in Lord Bernard. "Of course, yes, the man in whose house Ballantine was killed! You saw all about it in the accounts of the inquest, didn't you, Harry?"

Lord Henry shook his head. "I haven't the heart to read the papers nowadays," he said gloomily.

Lord Bernard took the letter and scanned it rapidly.

"But look here," he said, "you must remember something about it, surely?"

"Not a thing, I tell you," repeated Lord Henry. "Not a thing. I've signed so many things one way and another. . . ." His voice trailed off despairingly.

"But the date," persisted Lord Bernard. "October the thirteenth. What were you doing then?"

Lord Henry stared stupidly in front of him for a moment. Mallett said nothing. Since, contrary to his expectations, Lord Bernard seemed disposed to be a help rather than a hindrance, he was well content to let him do his work for him. Besides, it seemed more likely that Lord Henry would respond to his brother's methods than to any enquiries from a stranger. He waited therefore, while Ballantine's late colleague strove painfully to search his cloudy memory.

"Have a drink," suggested Lord Bernard.

Lord Henry obediently took a deep draught from the glass before him. Some colour came into his grey cheeks, and a look almost of intelligence into his eyes.

"I might have it down in my book," he said at last with the air of one who makes a great discovery.

He pulled from his pocket a small engagement book, and fluttered the leaves.

"Thirteenth—no, there's nothing there," he said. "Oh—I'm sorry—I was looking at September. October, now. . . . Here we are. Oh, yes, of course. Board meeting."

"A board meeting?" said Mallett. "Of the London and Imperial Estates Company?"

"Yes—it says so here."

"You signed this letter at a board meeting?"

"I suppose so."

"But why? Who asked you to?"

"That's just it. I don't expect anybody asked me to. There'd be a lot of papers in front of me, cheques and letters and so on, and I'd just sign along the dotted line."

"Without reading what you signed?"

"There wasn't time you know," answered Lord Henry. "Ballantine was generally in a hurry to get the business through. Besides I shouldn't have understood them if I had. So we just signed—the other directors and myself. 'Theirs not to reason why,' you know."

"Like a society beauty signing a soap advertisement," murmured Lord Bernard.

"Oh, shut up!" said his wretched brother. "It's easy

enough to talk like that now, but it seemed all right at the time." He turned to Mallett. "So there it is, you see," he groaned. "I know no more who this James is than the man in the moon."

But Mallett had not finished yet.

"Tell me," he said, "what was the usual procedure at your board meetings? You say you signed what was in front of you. How did it get there?"

"The stuff was generally just dealt round by that secretary fellow, Du Pine," was the reply. "What used to happen as a rule was this: we'd all go into the board room and sit round a long table, Ballantine at the top with a wad of papers in front of him, and Du Pine at his elbow, with another wad. Well, we'd have the minutes of the last meeting—you know the sort of thing—and then there'd be a lot of resolutions. Ballantine would propose something, Hartigan usually seconded, and we'd all say 'Aye'. There was hardly ever any discussion that I can remember. Du Pine would note it all down in his book as it went along. Then Ballantine and Du Pine generally had a little quiet conference at the head of the table, while the rest of us took a breather for a smoke and a chat, and then the papers and things to be signed would all come round. Du Pine would put down a bunch of half a dozen or so in front of each of us, according to how much business there was to be done, and we all signed our names. Then a box of cigars would come down the table, we'd each take one, and that was that. As soon as we'd lighted up, we trickled off, leaving those two to clear up the mess. Mind you," he added, "I don't swear that that was what happened this particular time, but it was what always did happen, so I expect it probably did."

"Then we can't even be sure that this letter was signed on the thirteenth of October?" Mallett pursued.

"Oh, yes, we can," answered Lord Henry confidently. "That was one thing I always made certain of—the dates. You see, it was the only thing I could make sure of understanding. Come to think of it, I tripped up rather badly once when I altered a date which was wrong. It seemed that it had been put wrong on purpose—some dirty work of Ballantine's, I suppose—and my putting it right again messed the whole show up. There was quite a stink about it. After that, I don't remember getting one that wasn't dated correctly."

"Only one more question," said the inspector. "All these documents which were put before you for signature would be typed in the office, I suppose?"

"Lord, yes! We had hosts of girls. Some jolly good lookers among 'em, too."

"Then you ought to be able to find the machine that typed this particular letter," put in Lord Bernard.

Mallett frowned. The idea had, of course, occurred to him, but he did not relish the suggestion that anyone could teach him his business.

"Proper enquiries will be made," he said severely, and folding up the paper, put it carefully away. Then he stood up.

"That is all I have to ask you, Lord Henry," he said. "Thank you for your assistance."

"But we can't let you go like this!" cried Lord Bernard. "You haven't even had a drink yet!"

"I never drink before meals, thanks," replied the inspector austerely.

"Quite right—it's a silly habit," Lord Bernard warmly agreed. "But you do have meals, I suppose? Then why not stay on here, and have a bite with us?"

As if in support of his plea, a delicious smell of cooking was wafted from the kitchen near by to where they sat. The inspector's resolution weakened, but he resisted temptation.

"I'm afraid I must be back in London tonight," he said.

"So must I," was the answer. "If you'll stop and dine with us, I'll run you back. My car's outside."

"Was that your car at the station, then?" asked Mallett.

"Did you notice her?" said Lord Bernard with animation. "Yes—that's mine. I left her down here last week. Some miserable learner on the front caved a mudguard in, and I came down to see my brother and bring her back. She's a Visconti-Sforza, you know—supercharged. You'd like her."

Mallett combined a man's appetite for food with a childish passion for speed. The joint appeal was irresistible.

"I'd like to very much," he said. "But what about my clothes?"

"That's all right," said Lord Henry, unexpectedly coming to life again. "Dine in the gallery of the restaurant. Needn't dress there. Watch the dancing. There are some devilish pretty girls here."

"That's settled, then," said Lord Bernard, and the party broke up, to reassemble later for the meal.

Before rejoining his hosts, Mallett put through a telephone call to Scotland Yard. He briefly told Frant of the new developments and gave instructions for specimens of the work of all the typewriters at the offices of the London and Imperial Estates Company to be secured as soon as possible. Then he asked for news.

"Nothing fresh has happened," was the reply, "unless you count that Mrs. Eales was seen in Bond Street today with her husband, which is a record, by all accounts. But someone is very anxious to see you as soon as he can. Most urgent, he says."

"Who is that?" asked the inspector.

"Fanshawe."

110

"Oh!" said Mallet. "Did he say why?"

"No."

"Thanks. I'll see about it." He rang off and made his way to the restaurant gallery, deep in thought.

He found the brothers already at table, and the meal ordered. A gold-topped bottle stood ready in its ice-pail. Lord Bernard indicated it with an apology.

"I hope you don't mind," he said. "It's not stuff I care about in the ordinary way. There's an air of artificial gaiety about it which always depresses me in the end. That's why it's so peculiarly appropriate at weddings." (Lord Bernard's matrimonial misadventures, Mallett was reminded, were notorious.) "But on an occasion like this, I think it is indicated. It will help us to cheer my brother up."

Mallett could not but smile at thus finding himself in a conspiracy to restore the spirits of a man who had quite certainly been implicated, however ignorantly, in a colossal fraud, and who had laid himself under suspicion of being privy to a murder. But he adapted himself to the odd situation with a good grace and settled down to enjoy his dinner.

It did not prove difficult. Lord Henry, as his brother had predicted, brightened considerably under the influence of the champagne, and if his contributions to the conversation consisted mainly of somewhat scabrous anecdotes, they were at least amusing, and to Mallett, whose learning did not lie in that direction, had the merit of being new. As for Lord Bernard, he was not only a good talker but, more surprisingly, a good listener. He seemed unaffectedly glad of the inspector's company and interested in what he had to say. It was obviously as unusual an experience for him to be dining with a detective as it was for Mallett to dine with the son of a marquis, and he seemed as pleased with his unaccustomed acquaintance

111

as a child with a new toy. He listened with flattering interest to all that the inspector had to tell him of his past cases, and punctuated the recital with shrewd and racy comment. Sooner or later, as it was bound to do, the conversation turned on Ballantine. Here Mallett discreetly fell silent, but Lord Bernard had plenty to say.

"It's easy to be wise after the event," he remarked, "but I always distrusted that man. Exactly why, it would be difficult to say. In my amateurish way, I make it my business to study people, and to do that I try to get on with people. I could never begin to get on with him. He was always very agreeable when one met him, he was intelligent and amusing to talk to, but there was always something about him that put me off." He pondered the problem for a moment or two, and then said seriously: "I think it was his clothes, chiefly."

"His clothes?" said Mallett in surprise.

"Yes. Clothes are an important part of one's life, you know, and Ballantine's clothes distinctly told me something about him which I didn't like. It's difficult to put into words, but there it is."

"Surely", said the inspector, "one of the advantages of being very rich is that you can wear exactly what you like. I've heard of lots of millionaires who dressed like tramps."

"Exactly," said Lord Bernard, "but what if you find a millionaire—or a man who's supposed to be a millionaire—who is always, consistently, too well dressed? Perhaps that's the wrong phrase—you are either well dressed or not—overdressed, shall I say? The impression that Ballantine always gave me was that of a man who had dressed himself for a part, the part of a great captain of business, and overdone it. And that, I suppose, bred the suspicion that he wasn't genuine, but merely an actor all the time."

"You're laying down the law a lot," grumbled Lord Henry, "but damn it, you didn't see very much of the man yourself."

"Quite a bit," his brother answered, "I was continually running up against him—at race meetings, and so on."

"Well, of course he'd dress up for a race meeting; who doesn't?"

"Yes, but it wasn't only at races. He was just the same at other times. Don't you remember, Harry, when you took us down to his place in Sussex for the annual office staff beano, what a sight he looked? They ran a rather good dramatic society," he explained to Mallett, "and I got up a little play they were doing for the occasion. And that reminds me—"

He paused to knock the ash off his cigar, and Mallett, contentedly puffing at his own, waited absently for the fact of which Lord Bernard had been reminded. It did not come. Instead, there was a loud ejaculation from his other side.

"By George!" exclaimed Lord Henry. "There's a real good looker down there at last!"

Human nature being what it is, a live good looker is always a more attractive subject than a dead financier. By common consent, the topic of Ballantine was abandoned, and the three men craned over the balcony to see.

In the restaurant beneath them, the tables had been filling up as they talked, and already the early diners were beginning to dance on the oval floor in the centre of the room. It was one of these that Lord Henry indicated— a tall fair girl in a white dress, with a mass of short-cut chestnut hair. She was pretty with a more than merely conventional prettiness, in part, perhaps, because she was so obviously radiantly happy. With sparkling eyes and lips parted in ecstasy, she danced as if she wished she need never stop.

Lord Henry twisted round in his chair to get a better view. He stared for some time before he spoke. Then he said: "Jenkinson!"

"Eh?" said his brother.

"Jenkinson. That's the name. Couldn't get my tongue to it at first. Her father lives near here. Retired soldier—general or something. With me at Harrow."

"Well, Miss Jenkinson seems pretty pleased with life this evening," Lord Bernard remarked.

"Umph! You mean, pleased with the young feller she's with," grunted Lord Henry.

Mallett had taken no part in this conversation. Beyond casually glancing at Miss Jenkinson and noting the fact that she was pretty, he paid no attention to her. He was considerably more interested in "the young feller" dancing with her.

"Who is he, d'you know?" said Lord Bernard's voice in his ear.

"Haven't an earthly." Lord Henry turned back to his liqueur.

But Mallett, his attention now thoroughly aroused, continued to watch. For here within a few yards of him, dancing contentedly in one of the most expensive hotels in England, was young Harper—Harper the superior estate agent's clerk, whose father had lost all his money five years ago, who had thrown up his job that morning without apparent cause, who. . . .

The inspector's thoughts raced. Acting on a sudden impulse, he rose, asked his hosts to excuse him and left the table. He came down the stairs just as the dance was ending and the couples were drifting back to their seats. Then a curious incident occurred. Harper's bow tie, inexpertly tied, had become disarranged, and the ends were hanging loose. The girl, with a laugh, began to tie it for him where they stood within a few feet of the watching detective. It was a pretty sight, but the bow that she had tied was scarcely a thing of beauty. Harper evidently felt that something was wrong and turned to rearrange it in one of the mirrors that flanked the wall. In order to do this, he half turned his back on the inspector, who looking carefully over his shoulder could see his face reflected quite clearly. Their eyes met, and as they did so Mallett saw something that almost made him start. It was the expression on the young man's face—a fleeting look of mingled fear and horror that he could not have believed possible in that handsome carefree countenance. The whole affair was over in an instant. Harper recovered himself almost at once, the bow was retied to his satisfaction, and he turned again to his partner with a smile. Then the lights were dimmed, the orchestra struck up a waltz, and they were in each other's arms once more. Mallett remained in the shadows, staring and wondering.

A hand fell on his shoulder.

"Well," said Lord Bernard's voice. "If you're ready, shall we be off?"

"Thanks," Mallett answered. "I think I've seen all I want to here."

Lord Bernard raised his eyebrows, but said nothing. It was characteristic of him not to ask what the inspector had seen, or why he had left the table so abruptly. Clearly he was a man who could keep his own counsel and respect that of others. Silently he followed his guest out of the hotel and into the waiting car.

"It's a new experience to have a policeman in the car with me," said Lord Bernard as they passed the pylons which mark the boundary of Brighton. "Up till now they've always been on the other side of the fence, so to speak. D'you mind if I let her out a bit?"

Mallett did not mind. The rush through the darkened countryside over a road gleaming fantastically white in the headlamps was exhilarating. The Visconti-Sforza, he was glad to observe, was not one of those pseudo-racing cars which seek to give an impression of speed by making a noise like an old-fashioned aeroplane. It ran silkily, silently—and fast. The inspector leaned back in his cushioned seat and luxuriated in the pace. Lord Bernard, like most good drivers, was not given to talk while at the wheel, and the journey was accomplished for the most part in silence. Mallett had had a long and tiring day, but now as the car sped on, he found his thoughts speeding too, as though to keep up with it.

He concentrated his mind on the mysterious letter of recommendation to the bank, which had brought him down to Brighton. In a sense, he had been disappointed, in that the signatory had been able to tell him next to nothing about it. But was it really such a disappointment after all? He had never suspected—no sane person ever would have suspected—that the amiable nobleman he had just interviewed would prove to be concerned in the murder of the man whose innocent tool he had been. Nobody, of course, could be wholly exempt from suspicion in a case such as this, but, so far as he, Mallett, was concerned, he accepted without reservation his account of the board meeting and what went on there. And that account was, after all, of considerable value. It meant that somebody in the London and Imperial Estates Office had successfully endeavored to get a director to vouch for Colin James. It seemed clear that most of the board took their duties as lightly as Lord Henry, and it was probably the merest chance that it was his signature that happened to appear on the letter. His mind went back to Lord Henry's description of the procedure—Ballantine with a big wad of papers in front of him, Du Pine with another. From which set of documents had this one come? He toyed for a moment with the theory that one of the other directors might have contrived to shuffle it into Lord Henry's pile unobserved, but dismissed it as improbable. Remained then, the chairman and the secretary. Whichever it was, one thing was clear. Either was perfectly competent himself to recommend a client to the good offices of a bank. That it should have been done in this roundabout way led to only one conclusion—that the real author of the letter was anxious that his connection with James should not come to light. And this, he remembered, was the first time that his name had appeared at all—the birth, so to speak, of Colin James, who was to walk away into blank space a bare month later along the pavement of the Avenue Magenta, leaving a corpse behind him in Kensington. On the face of it, it did not seem probable that Ballantine had assisted him. Men are not usually privy to their own murder. On the other hand, there must be some connection, as yet unestablished, between the two, or how did Ballantine come to go, apparently of his own free will, to the house where he met his death? There were, he knew, many dark corners in the financier's life which had yet to be cleared up. Perhaps James was a <u>jackal</u> of his and privy to some of his less reputable activities, who knowing that Ballantine's time was running short had seized the opportunity to make away with him and with the spoil which he had prepared for his flight?

Mallett pulled at his moustache and frowned. No, that didn't seem quite to fit the case either. For if James had been working for Ballantine it must have been for some time past. By October Ballantine must have known that a crisis in his affairs was approaching. And yet it was in October that, according to this theory, he began to interest himself in James's affairs. He turned to the other possibility—Du Pine. All that he had seen of the man and all that he had heard of him led him to believe that he was capable of most things. He had been Ballantine's confidant and assistant in large and complex operations—therefore he was intelligent; he had been a partner to his frauds, therefore unscrupulous. But what could his motive have been for engineering his employer's murder? Scarcely robbery. If he had been anxious to get a share in the booty which Ballantine intended to make off with, a little judicious blackmail would have served his turn, and, the inspector judged, would have been more in character than the brutal expedient of killing him. Besides, there was still the initial difficulty of solving the problem of how Ballantine came to go to James's house. If Du Pine were responsible for James establishing himself in Daylesford Gardens, that only removed one stage further the missing connection between Ballantine and James. There could be no doubt, from his demeanour at the inquest, that the secretary was thoroughly frightened, but of what? Perhaps merely of whatever shady actions of his might come to light in the records of the "Twelve Apostles." Possibly—but if he stood to lose by the exposure of Ballantine's financial crookedness he would be the less likely to commit a crime which would make its discovery doubly certain. If Du Pine had plotted Ballantine's death he would surely have had the common prudence to make his own position secure beforehand.

Casting back in his mind, he recollected something else about Du Pine—his dramatic introduction of the name of Fanshawe at the inquest. Was it a blind? If so, it was a singularly unskillful one. For he must have known that the police would not be long in discovering that James had been vouched for by the company a full month before Fanshawe was released from prison. That was yet another argument against attributing the authorship of the letter to him. Had Du Pine said the truth about Fanshawe's visit to the office? Well, Fanshawe could help to clear that up himself. But why blurt the name out in the most public way possible, instead of quietly informing the police as any reasonable man would have done? It was almost as if he wanted to concentrate attention on Fanshawe and away from himself. Why? Or alternatively, perhaps he genuinely believed that Fanshawe had taken vengeance on Ballantine, and feared a like fate for himself in return for his share in the events of five years ago. On the whole, that theory seemed most plausible, but it left the mystery of the letter as deep as ever.

"What a fool I am!" Mallett said to himself. "Why don't I practise what I preach? Here I am, theorizing without the facts, when a simple examination of the office typewriters will give me all I want—that is, if the girl who took the letter down has any memory."

He deliberately relaxed, and let his thoughts wander. Links, he reflected vaguely, missing links—the case was full of them. And he was going to see Fanshawe tomorrow. And the only link between Fanshawe and James was—Harper of all people! Fanshawe had been a friend of Harper's father, and Harper had found James his house—it seemed remote enough in all conscience! The personalities in the drama began to flit through his tiring brain like colours in a kaleidoscope. The speed of the car, from being a stimulant, became a narcotic. He dozed. Presently he found himself speaking to Harper who vainly tried to tie a bow, and explained that if he didn't get it straight he would be murdered, while Lord

Bernard shouted in his ear: "You mustn't be over-dressed! It's a crime to be over-dressed!"

He jerked himself awake. Lord Bernard was still speaking, but what he said was: "We're just coming into London. Where can I drop you?"

15

Mr. Colin James

"Are you sure there were no other machines in the office?" Mallett asked Frant.

It was Friday morning, and they sat together in the inspector's room at Scotland Yard, at a table littered with little typewritten slips.

"Absolutely," was the reply. "They were all of the same make—big office typewriters, except for a small portable in Du Pine's room. That was a 'Diadem'."

"And quite obviously *this* wasn't," rejoined Mallett, tapping the letter with a broad forefinger. "I don't pretend to be an expert in these matters, but at a guess I should say it was a light Hornington."

He crumpled up the slips into a ball and threw them into the waste-paper basket with a shrug of disgust.

"And that's that!" he observed. "Now where do we stand? Here we have a letter written on office-paper but not in the office—brought in from outside so that poor dear Gaveston could sign it. Who could get at the paper? Obviously, anyone employed in the office who cared to sneak a bit and take it home with him. Who

121

owned a typewriter? Nowadays nearly everybody does. By the way, I wonder if Du Pine has one at his private house?"

"He certainly has," said Frant, with an air of triumph. "Here's a specimen of its work."

He laid a sheet of notepaper before the inspector, adding:

"It was addressed to the Chief Commissioner personally. It has just been sent down for us to deal with."

My Lord,
Having applied several times in vain at my local police station, I am constrained to write to you personally and ask for police protection. As you may be aware, I was, until it ceased to carry on business, the secretary of the London and Imperial Estates Company Limited. Since giving evidence at the inquest on my late chairman, Mr. Ballantine, I have every reason to suppose that my life also is in danger. I have more than once observed some extremely suspicious characters prowling near my house. There is one on the pavement opposite to me as I write. I earnestly beg that my request, which in the circumstances I feel sure you will agree is no more than reasonable, may be attended to without delay.

> I am, my lord,
> Your obedient servant,
> H. DU PINE.

Mallett placed the letter side by side with the other. "A different make of machine altogether," he commented. "Just look at the tail of the 'g's' for instance. Well, what do you suggest we do about this?"

"Take off our men, and put on uniformed constables,"

said Frant promptly. "The suspicious characters were our own people, of course."

Mallett pondered. "I think we can do better than that," he replied after a pause. "Keep the same men on, but put them into uniform for the occasion. That will kill two birds with one stone. We shall be watching him then without his knowing it, and giving him what he wants at the same time."

"I don't quite see—" Frant began.

"Don't you? Well, just think it over for a bit. What is the job of a constable who is told off to give somebody or other house police protection? Obviously to watch any suspicious person who may appear outside the house, or who may approach somebody. But it isn't to watch the behaviour of that somebody himself, is it? Nor is it part of his job to see what goes on in the house. There's a very considerable difference. And I'll tell you another thing, Frant. The average crook is apt to have a healthy respect for a plainclothes detective, but very little for the uniformed officer. He thinks of him as an ornament in the streets, just something to control traffic and arrest pickpockets, and so on. If Du Pine thinks he is being protected by ordinary flat-footed coppers he'll be much more likely to give himself away than if he's afraid he has a detective on his heels—that is if he has anything to give away."

"Certainly he hasn't done anything to give himself away yet," Frant remarked.

"Perhaps he wasn't quite satisfied in his mind about the 'suspicious characters'," said Mallett with a grin. "Now I've something else to tell you."

He briefly told the sergeant of what he had seen on the dancing-floor of the Riviera Hotel.

"Odd, very odd," said Frant, when he had done. "And the oddest part of it, if I may say so, is not that he should

123

have been frightened at seeing you—"

"Thanks," said Mallett.

"I mean he would naturally connect you with the murder, which must have been a horrible shock to him—"

"He seemed pretty cool about it when I saw him. That was one of the things that struck me at the time. But you were going to say—"

"What really seems strange is that all of a sudden he could afford to be in a place like that. Do you know what they charge you for dinner there?"

"I do not," said Mallett with relish. "I didn't have to pay the bill, thank goodness."

"Well, believe me, sir, it's something terrific. How could he possibly run to it, I want to know?"

"What do we know about Harper's position, anyway?" Mallett asked.

"Quite a lot sir," answered Frant, eager to prove his own industry. "We have his address, you know, down Ealing way. I got into touch with the police there, and I find he lives alone with his mother—most respectable, but as poor as the devil. A tiny house, a servant who comes in twice a week—you know the sort of thing. It doesn't go with posh hotels at Brighton at all."

"Poor young men have gone bust now and then before this," said the inspector. "But you're quite right, all the same, Frant. This boy has come into money, or the near prospect of it, just lately. I'll tell you what makes me sure: the expression of the girl he was dancing with."

"I don't see that," Frant objected. "Of course she'd be pleased to be dancing with a boy she was fond of."

"But she wasn't just 'pleased'," persisted Mallett. "She was completely happy—without a care in the world. You don't so often see people like that, and there was no mistaking it. Now just consider the—what d'you call it—the psychology of it. Here's a girl who's been in love

124

with a young man for some time—you'll remember what Mr. Browne said—who hasn't a penny to bless himself with; obviously no prospect of getting married for years and years. Would she look like that just because she was spending one evening with him, which anyway she knew he couldn't possibly afford?"

"Lots of girls are never so happy as when they're making a chap spend a month's wages in an evening," remarked Frant sagely.

"Not that sort of girl," said the inspector emphatically.

When people say "Not that sort of girl," particularly when they say it about a girl you have not yourself seen, there is obviously nothing to be said, and the sergeant accordingly remained silent.

"Why not simply interview him and ask him where his money comes from?" he said finally.

Mallett shook his head.

"No," he said. "I've frightened this fellow pretty badly already, without meaning to. If he's got anything to conceal, he'll have done it by now, and have his story pat and ready. If there's nothing fishy about it after all, there's no harm done."

"Then why not ask the girl, or her father, and see what they know about him?"

"That's all very well, Frant, but you can't just stroll into a man's house, and say: 'I'm a police officer, and I want to know how much money your daughter's fiancé has got and how he got it'—can you? At least, I shouldn't care to do it, especially with a retired general. All the same, I should very much like to have the chance of a talk with him."

"And his daughter," added Frant, but under his breath.

The inspector drummed on the table for a moment, tugging at his moustache with his disengaged hand.

"Still," he murmured, "it might be managed. It's a long shot, but it might come off. I think I'll have a talk on the phone with the Sussex police."

"Now, or after lunch?" asked Frant, who knew his superior's weakness.

"After lunch, of course," said Mallett with decision. "Let's see, Fanshawe's coming here at three, isn't he? Well, I'm not going to interview him on an empty stomach, if I can help it. There's nothing else, is there?"

"There's a big bunch of reports from all over the country about people resembling James," answered the sergeant. "I suppose they'll all have to be enquired into, but not one of them looks the least helpful."

A description of James based upon the evidence already obtained and described with the usual euphemism as that of "a man whom the police desire to interview" had been circulated. These were just beginning to bear fruit, and the resulting harvest was, as Frant said, an unpromising one. Mysterious stout men with beards seemed to have appeared all at once in every part of England. They had been seen leaping into taxis, disappearing down subways, lurking suspiciously behind the hedges of country lanes. Late at night, they had drunk hasty cups of tea at London coffee-stalls or cadged lifts from lorry-drivers on arterial roads. They had even been seen, faces in the dark, peering through the windows of blameless suburban residences. Every one of them, Mallett knew, was probably the product of mere hysteria, begotten of an urge to figure in the news; but somewhere in the heap of nonsense might lurk the one grain of information that would make all the difference. Therefore it would all have to be sifted, enquired into, patiently and relentlessly, until its worthlessness was proved.

Mallett looked at the bulging file and then at his watch.

"Not now," he said. "Have you ever noticed, Frant, how a big dinner the night before gives you an appetite for lunch next day?"

"I can't say that I have," answered Frant.

"Really, I have, often. I'm off now. These things must wait. I feel so hungry that I shouldn't care to stop if Mr. James stepped into the room this minute."

There was a knock at the door.

"Yes, yes, what is it?"

An officer put his head round the door.

"Excuse me, sir," he said, "but there's a man here who's very anxious to see you at once. He says his name is Colin James."

Mallett sank back into his chair.

"I take it all back," he gasped.

Whatever anxiety Mr. James may have had to visit Scotland Yard, it was apparent that once there he found himself in a state of great embarrassment. He stood in the doorway of Mallett's room, shifting his heavy weight from one foot to another, and turning watery blue eyes first on Mallett, then on Frant, and finally on a vacant spot midway between them. He was palpably in a miserably nervous state, and looked as though an incautious sound or movement would send him bolting back through the door again.

"Won't you sit down, sir?" cooed the inspector in his blandest tones. "I understand you have something to tell me?"

The visitor lowered himself into a chair, where he perched diffidently on the extreme edge.

"I—I really must apologize for troubling you in this way," he began, "but I feel it my duty in the *very* peculiar circumstances—it is all most unusual, I have never had anything to do with the police before and—but my name has been mentioned—excuse me!"

His face was momentarily obscured by a large blue and white chequered handkerchief, while a sneeze exploded like a bomb in the quiet room.

"I beg your pardon," resumed Mr. James when his face reappeared from its momentary eclipse. "A nasty cold— a very nasty cold. I shouldn't really have travelled in this weather—my daughter tried to dissuade me, but I felt it my duty—"

This time the sneeze took him by surprise, and Mallett ducked hastily to avoid the resultant shower. So far the inspector had said nothing. Indeed he had only listened with half an ear to the disjointed utterances of the stranger. But his eyes had been busy, and his brain was mechanically registering what he saw, and checking and comparing it with what he had heard elsewhere. The first impression produced by Mr. James was one of great size. As he sat, uncomfortably far forward in his chair, his stomach protruded almost to the desk behind which the inspector sheltered. The impression of size was reinforced by the bushy brown beard that straggled over his chest. But above the beard there showed itself not the fat florid face that one might have been expecting from a man of such bulk, but a peaky little countenance, with sunken cheeks and hollow eyes. His limbs, too, were by comparison thin. One wondered how such inadequate legs could support the burden of his body. "He looks like a thin man badly made up to play Falstaff," thought Mallett. He remembered Harper's words: "A fat man— or rather, paunchy. He had a big stomach and a thin face, as if he had a bad digestion."

Aloud he said: "Now let's take this quietly, Mr.— James. That is your name, I think?"

The visitor plunged into a pocket and produced a grimy card. "That's me," he said.

The inspector read: "Colin James, 14 Market Street,

Great Easington, Norfolk." In the bottom left-hand corner were added the words: "Seed and Corn Merchant."

"Well?" he asked. "What have you got to do with this affair?"

"That's exactly it!" cried Mr. James. "What indeed? I'm a respectable man, sir, always have been. You can ask anybody in Easington, or for miles round—as far as Norwich if you like."

"But you thought you'd like to come as far as London to make sure," put in Mallett drily. Any hopes he had of hearing anything useful from the new arrival began to disappear. It seemed that Colin James in the flesh would prove to be no more value than the unsubstantial rumours which filled his files.

Mr. James blew his nose with a trumpet-like blast.

"I'm sorry if I've troubled you," he said sorrowfully. "I thought it right to come as soon as I could. My daughter told me it wouldn't be any good to anyone, but it seemed wrong not to. So as soon as my cold would let me get out of the house, I did"—he sniffed—"though I was hardly fit to travel as it was."

The inspector was touched in spite of himself.

"I'm afraid it is you who have been troubled, Mr. James," he said.

"I wouldn't mind that, sir," answered James, "if I thought I'd been of any use. But I can tell you, it takes a good deal to get me out of my home nowadays—quite apart from this cold of mine, I mean. My health isn't what it was, you know. I suffer a good deal—"

"From your digestion?" enquired Mallett.

"My digestion, just so. I wonder how you guessed that, sir. It's easy to see you're not a detective for nothing."

"Well, we're trained to notice things, you know," said the inspector pleasantly, rising as he spoke. "Thank you for coming, Mr. James. I think it's clear you're not the man we are looking for."

"Oh, you can be sure of that, sir," the corn merchant assured him earnestly. "But it was a funny coincidence, wasn't it? My name and beard and figure and all, my digestion, too, for all I knew, though you didn't put that in the description."

"I think I can promise you that your digestion alone would acquit you," said Mallett gravely.

"Would it really, now? That is most interesting—most interesting. I should never have thought of that. It just shows the way you gentlemen of Scotland Yard work. Well, all I can say is, in that case, I ought to have a good alibi—if that's the word—for any crimes. That's the first good thing I've known come of my wretched stomach. It spoils all pleasure in life"—he contemplated his great paunch gravely—"it does indeed. The least little thing upsets it. You ask my daughter what happened when she took me to France."

"Oh, you went to France?" asked Mallett, "When was that?"

"Last August it was. A week in Paris. She was bent on our going, and all because the Edwardses up the street had been there at Easter and she wanted to be even with them. And nothing would content her but that I should come too. Never again, that's all I say—never again!"

"You don't happen to have your passport with you by any chance, I suppose?"

"There I go again!" exclaimed Mr. James violently, dropping back into the chair from which he had just painfully risen. "Forgetting the one thing I meant to tell you. Not but what my daughter said it was all nonsense—"

"Never mind about your daughter," said Mallett. "What was it you wanted to tell us about your passport?"

"It was stolen, sir—or at any rate, I lost it, and I always maintained it was stolen, though what anyone should want with such a thing I could never make out."

"Stolen? How?"

"On the way home. I had it in my hand at Dover, of that I'm sure, because I remember passing it to the man in the office place and he never looked at it but just pushed it back to me. And then by the time we got to the train—my hands were full of things—tickets and parcels and a penny for an evening paper—you know how it is—anyhow, when I came to look for it, it wasn't there."

"Did you make any complaint at the time?"

"No. I looked for it on the platform, you know, just casually. I remember I said to my daughter: 'My passport's gone', and she said: 'You ought to tell the police', but I said: 'Nonsense, I shan't want the thing again as long as I live—you're not going to drag me abroad to face that dreadful cooking any more, you can be sure of that,' I said—"

"All this on the platform, where anyone could hear you, I suppose?"

"Just so, sir, I suppose anyone could, though I never thought of that at the time."

"You could hardly be expected to think that someone would pick it up, borrow your name and appearance, live under that name for a month and then use the passport to escape from justice after committing murder, certainly," said Mallett.

"Good heavens, is that what the rascal did?" exclaimed Mr. James.

"It looks very much like it."

"God bless my soul, I didn't know there were such people in the world—I didn't really. It gives me quite a turn to think of it."

"Well, you've given us something to think about," answered the inspector, "and we are much obliged to you. Now, Mr. James, to make everything regular, I'll ask you to wait here for a few moments while Sergeant Frant puts your story into writing, and then you can go back to nurse your cold at Easington. One other thing you can do for us," he added. "Do you mind if we take your photograph before you go? It may be valuable for our purposes."

"Not in the least," Mr. James assured him.

"See that that is done," he said to Frant. "I have an important appointment outside now. When you have taken this gentleman's statement, telephone to the police station at Easington and verify what he has told us about himself. Good day, Mr. James."

He departed to his lunch, leaving the sergeant, whose meal-times were not considered of importance, gloomily manipulating a fountain-pen.

16

Fanshawe Speaks

Friday, November 20th

It was afternoon. The Easington police had vouched for the bona fides of Colin James, and he had returned to his corn and seeds. Another visitor was now awaited, and for him the stage was set with more than ordinary care. A comfortable low chair was provided for him, for the inspector had found by experience that men talk with greater fluency when they are at ease, and at the same time the questioner has an advantage if he is sitting above the person he is interrogating. "If they put witnesses down in the well of the court instead of sticking them up in box level with the judge, there'd be much less perjury," he used to say. This chair was arranged so that it faced the light, and at the same time an open box of good cigarettes was placed within easy reach on the corner of the inspector's desk. At the other end of the room a shorthand writer was in unobtrusive attendance.

When all was settled to Mallet's satisfaction there was still some time to wait. An uneasy air of expectancy descended on the room. Frant, whose nerves were less under control than his superior's, found the silence hard to bear.

"What do you think he's coming here to tell us?" he said.

"I haven't the least idea," was the answer. "I shouldn't be surprised if it turns out to be something completely unimportant after all. There are so many loose ends in this case that I'm beginning to wonder if we are ever going to find a thread that will lead us anywhere." He was silent for a moment, and then, as if feeling that the sergeant was finding the tension oppressive, began on another subject.

"What did you make of James's story?" he asked.

"I think we've learned something very valuable from it," Frant answered. "That name, description, passport—it can't be all coincidence."

"No, I agree, it's wildly unlikely that it should be. But you see what that leads us to. We have simply pushed back the beginning of the story a month or more further. It means that as early as August someone had made up his mind to impersonate Mr. James."

"He can't have known beforehand that he was going to pick up the passport," objected Frant.

"No, he couldn't. But having had the luck to find it, he must have seen at once the sort of use he could put to it—or why didn't he return it, or hand it to the police as any honest man would have done? More and more I'm becoming convinced that we have to deal with a very dangerous and intelligent man. You see, he is not only a careful plotter with a long view, but a man who can take a chance when it comes his way, and build it into his plans."

"Of course, we can't be sure that it was the same man who stole the passport and who afterwards used it," put in the sergeant. "Any crook might be glad of the chance to sneak such a thing, especially when he had reason to think it wouldn't be enquired after."

"And then to sell it to someone who saw what he could do with it? You may be right, Frant. But whichever way you look at it, it leaves us in the same miserable vagueness as ever. The fellow wanted a disguise—he took the easiest one that offered. A false beard is easy—a false stomach isn't much harder, if you come to think of it, especially if you want to impersonate a man with a thin face and a big body. Then in just the same way, he wants himself introduced to a bank by the company, and he so arranged it that any director out of half a dozen might sign the letter. We started off with two bits of positive evidence—that he called himself Colin James and that he was recommended by Lord Henry Gaveston, and neither the real James nor Gaveston can help us in the very least."

"And I don't see that *he*," Frant nodded to the door, "can possibly help us in that direction, either."

"Even supposing he wants to, which I somehow doubt," added Mallett. "What earthly knowledge can Fanshawe have of James?"

"The real one or the sham one, do you mean?"

"The sham one, of course. Call him James the Second, if you like."

"I think the Old Pretender would be more appropriate," said the sergeant.

Mallett wrinkled his nose, a sure sign that he was vexed. His schooling had not included much history, and he felt obscurely that his subordinate was showing off. But before he could think of a rejoinder, the door was thrown open, and Fanshawe was announced.

Four years of prison life had left but little mark upon the former chairman of Fanshawe's Bank. His complexion, always pale, was perhaps a shade whiter, his lean face just a trifle thinner still; otherwise Mallett could observe no change in the man he had last seen in the dock at the Old Bailey. The voice, too, when he spoke, was the same—quiet and cultured, always with a cynical undertone beneath the smooth surface, a hint of hidden fires kept resolutely under control. John Fanshawe was a very different type of man from the financier with whom his name had so often been coupled. A man of taste and refinement, he had lived in his days of prosperity aloof from the world. He had been able to enjoy riches without arrogance, just as he had met ruin and disgrace without whining. In good times and bad alike, he had been as if sustained by some hidden source of fortitude, an innate pride which never deserted him.

Mallett felt oddly abashed before this calm proud man, but Fanshawe put him at his ease at once.

"Good afternoon, Inspector," he began. "I think you have been promoted since we last met?"

"I have—yes," answered Mallett. "Good afternoon, Mr. Fanshawe."

Fanshawe lowered himself into the arm-chair and took a cigarette. "*Mr. Fanshawe!*" he murmured. "You have no idea how refreshing it is to recover one's individuality again! I wonder whether anybody who has not experienced it can know what it feels like to be a mere number. That is the real horror of prison life, Mallett, the sinking of one's identity in a herd of indistinguishable fellow creatures. 'He that filches from me my good name'," he quoted. "Well, thank heavens that is over, at all events!" He glanced round the room. "Forgive me," he went on, "but have not rather elaborate preparations been made to receive me? I mean—" he waved his hand at the stenographer in the corner—"it almost looks as though something in the nature of a public utterance was expected of me. I'm afraid you are likely to be disappointed."

"Perhaps it would save us both trouble if you said exactly what you have come here for," said Mallett severely.

"I apologize, Inspector," said Fanshawe, the irony in his voice making itself felt. "Your time is valuable I know. I shall waste very little of it. I have merely come to make a complaint. I want to know why I, a week after my release from jail, should still be subjected to the indignity and inconvenience of being shadowed by detectives."

Mallett found it hard to suppress a smile. It was a somewhat ludicrous coincidence that this request should follow so hard on Du Pine's plea for police protection. Aloud he said:

"You will understand, Mr. Fanshawe, that the circumstances are a little unusual."

"The only unusual aspect of the circumstances, as I understand them," answered Fanshawe, "is that on leaving prison I was expressly exempted from the ordinary regulations about reporting to the police and so forth. I presume that you are aware of that?"

"Certainly. I am given to understand that the order was made on the direct instructions of the Home Secretary. It was most exceptional."

"Personally, I think it is the least he could have done," said Fanshawe with a touch of hauteur. "I always treated him very decently when he was my fag at school."

"You must know perfectly well", said Mallett impatiently, "that the supervision you are complaining of has nothing whatever to do with anything that happened *before* you were released from prison."

"I understand you. I read the papers, like everyone else. I am to gather, then, that this inquisition has to do with the events of last week-end?"

"If you read the papers," answered the inspector, "you will have seen your own name mentioned in the reports of the inquest on Lionel Ballantine."

137

A strange smile lit up Fanshawe's lean face. "In that little rat Du Pine's evidence? I did indeed." He turned suddenly and looked the inspector full in the eyes. "May I ask whether you suspect me of this crime?" he asked.

"Nobody is free from suspicion in a case of this kind," replied Mallett gravely. "Now, Mr. Fanshawe, don't you think you could assist us by answering a few questions?"

"And if I refuse, as I have a perfect right to do?"

"Then I am afraid you will have to go to the Home Secretary and ask him to relieve you of police supervision, for I shall not take the responsibility myself."

Fanshawe blew a long jet of smoke from his mouth and very deliberately crushed the stub of his cigarette in an ashtray.

"Very well," he said at last. "I have no objection to telling you. Du Pine's statement is substantially true. I did call on Ballantine"—an involuntary spasm contracted his features as he pronounced the name—"last Friday morning. I contrived to get in by using a false name, and as soon as he saw who I was he had me turned out of the office. Not before I had told him just a little of what I thought of him, though."

"Yes?"

Fanshawe smiled. He had a delightful, even brilliant smile, though now it seemed to hold a hint of malice. "My dear Inspector," he said, "that was what you wished to know, was it not? I really don't see how I can help you any further."

Mallett folded his large hands and put them squarely on the desk in front of him. Looming over the figure that reclined in the easy chair he seemed strangely impressive, and his voice when it came had an urgency, a vibrant appeal that was rare in it.

"Don't let us beat about the bush any longer," he said. "I am going to be perfectly frank with you, and I want you to be frank with me. You are of all men alive the one who had the greatest motive for hating Ballantine. The day you were sentenced you threatened his life publicly. The day after you were released he was murdered. In the face of that you complain that you are watched by the police, while all the time you refuse to be frank with us."

"You must allow me to point out, Inspector," came the cold comment from the chair, "that this is the first opportunity I have had to 'be frank with you', as you put it."

Mallett felt that his impressive period had somehow missed fire. "I can't interview everyone at once," he muttered.

"Quite so, though no doubt you have able assistants to help you. Now, since I am here, entirely of my own volition, am I to understand that if I answer your questions the detectives will be withdrawn?"

"I can make no promises," Mallett answered. "That must depend on the extent to which you are able to satisfy us. But I should have thought that for an innocent man it would be natural to want to assist justice—"

"If by assisting justice you mean arresting the man who killed Ballantine"—again that curious spasm—"I shall do no such thing. He did a splendid thing which badly needed doing, and which I should have been only too glad to do myself."

The inspector tried another tack.

"Then in your own interest it is desirable that you should convince us that you had no hand in it," he said.

Fanshawe laughed aloud. "In the sacred name of self-interest, then!" he cried. "What do you want to know?"

"We will begin at the beginning," said Mallett. "Why did you go to see Ballantine on Friday morning?"

"Because he had ruined me—and not only me but a large number of people who had trusted me. It was

139

through supporting him and his schemes that my bank was destroyed. He got out in time—very neatly—and I was left, as the phrase goes, to carry the baby."

"And you went to see him in the hope of getting some repayment from him?"

"You might put it that way—yes."

"Very well. Now as to your movements during the rest of the day."

"What are the movements of a newly liberated prisoner in London, without friends or prospects? Mine were mostly on the tops of motor omnibuses. I drifted aimlessly round London all day, simply enjoying the sensation of being my own master again, and noticing all the changes since I had seen it last. And you have no idea how the place has changed in the last four years, Inspector. You could write a book on it."

"And then?"

"Then I went home to tea."

"What do you mean by home?"

Fanshawe winced. "That is rather crude, Inspector," he murmured. "Yes, you are right, of course. I have no home now. I mean my sister's flat."

"In Daylesford Court Mansions?"

"Yes. I know what you are going to say next. Within a couple of hundred yards of Daylesford Gardens. Odd, isn't it?" He smiled as though in pure enjoyment at the coincidence.

"And then?"

"Oh, then I packed my bag and went abroad."

"You went abroad that same day?"

"Certainly. That night, rather. By the Newhaven boat to Paris. My daughter is living there."

Mallett took this piece of information in complete calm, but Frant, unable to contain himself, let his breath escape in a prolonged whistle. Fanshawe turned his head in his direction and stared at him for a moment with raised eyebrows, but said nothing.

The inspector recalled his attention by asking quietly: "What class did you travel?"

"I bought a third-class return ticket in the City before I went to see—the person we have been discussing," was the answer. "Disgustingly uncomfortable, but beggars can't be choosers!"

"Did you notice anybody in particular travelling first-class?"

Fanshawe sat up abruptly. "Now look here," he said in a hard tone quite unlike his usual voice, "I have already told you that I am not interested in the ends of justice, if those ends are to avenge the killing of—Ballantine." He spat out the name with concentrated fury. "If anything I could say would help you to find the gentleman who called himself Colin James, I should not say it. If I could have shaken him by the hand for what he did, I should have done so."

It was Mallett's turn to be calm. "Very well," he said smoothly. "If that is your attitude, I shall not press you. You can tell me where you bought your ticket, I suppose?"

"Oh, yes, Rawson's in Cornhill. They know me there."

"Thank you. And while you were in Paris, I take it you stayed with your daughter?"

"Yes. She lives out at Passy." He gave the address.

"You went there at once on arriving in Paris?"

"No, of course I didn't. You get there at such an unearthly hour you couldn't possibly go to anyone's place, particularly if you weren't expected. I spent what was left of the night at a hotel close to the station—a vile place, the best I could afford. I've forgotten the name."

"Not the Hotel Du Plessis, by any chance?"

"Certainly not—I've never heard of the place."

Mallett paused for a full half-minute. Then he said: "And that is all you mean to tell us, Mr. Fanshawe?"

"That is all I have to tell you, Inspector Mallett."

"Good afternoon, then."

"Good afternoon. And will the detectives be withdrawn?"

"I can make no promises."

There was silence in the room for a space after he had gone. The shorthand writer took his notes and went out to prepare a transcript of the interview. Mallett sat staring at the blotter on his desk, mechanically pulling at his moustache, deep in thought. Finally he turned to Frant.

"Well, and what did you make of him?" he asked.

"Obviously a very conceited man," answered the sergeant.

"Conceited? H'm, yes, and a good deal more than that. But you're right, Frant. He is a very vain man indeed. Prison life hurt his vanity more than anything else, obviously. Has it ever occurred to you, Frant, that all murderers are exceptionally vain? You have to be, to think that your own interests or convenience are sufficiently important to justify killing a man."

"Then do you think—?"

"No, I don't. Not yet, anyway. There's not a thing he's told us which isn't consistent with perfect innocence, and not a jury in England would convict on it. So anyway, our private beliefs don't matter."

"My own private belief, for what it's worth," said Frant, "is that Fanshawe was in league with James. I look at it this way: James, for some reason or another, disguises himself as—James. He lives in that disguise, very likely from August onwards—certainly for a month. He scrapes acquaintance with Ballantine—that may be presumed from the letter to the bank. All this time, he is waiting for Fanshawe's release from prison. He engages a house through an old friend of Fanshawe's and has for his sole servant a man formerly employed by that old friend. Then immediately Fanshawe is free, he decoys Ballantine to the house—"

"Having first got rid of the dependable servant," interrupted Mallett. "Why?"

"That's natural enough. He didn't want a third person to be involved in the murder. I dare say he could trust him up to a point and not to give away his disguise, but letting him have a share in the crime is another thing."

"I see. Go on."

"Where was I? He decoys Ballantine to his house, where Fanshawe is already concealed. Together they kill him, leave the place separately, and travel over to France by the same boat but, for safety's sake, by different classes."

"If your theory is right," the inspector objected, "it doesn't account for one rather odd fact. Why did Fanshawe, who was in league with James to kill Ballantine in Daylesford Gardens, bother to go to Lothbury on Friday morning and draw attention to himself by threatening him in his own office?"

"Perhaps," said Frant, "he didn't then know of James's plans. Communication with a prisoner isn't easy, and it may be that it wasn't until later in the day that he got into touch with James and knew of the preparations that had been made."

"That doesn't seem very plausible to me," the inspector answered. "I think we're agreed that everything we have discovered so far points to a carefully arranged crime. James wouldn't have laid his plans so thoroughly and left himself such a small margin of time, if he'd thought that Fanshawe wasn't going to do his part properly. Don't forget that the lease of the house was nearly up, and the tickets for France bought already. It seems to me more likely that the two were in touch with each other while Fanshawe was still in Maidstone."

"Then what's your explanation of Fanshawe's behaviour on Friday morning—assuming my theory is right?"

"Assuming that your theory is right—and after all we are only dealing in assumptions—don't you think it possible that Fanshawe's visit to Ballantine was all part of the plan?"

"In what way?"

"You have suggested that James decoyed Ballantine to his house in Daylesford Gardens. You haven't suggested how he managed it."

"No, that's a weak spot in the theory, I admit."

"That is one weak spot, and the threat to Ballantine on Friday morning is another. Let's see if the two can't cancel each other out. Suppose James sent Fanshawe to frighten Ballantine? We know, and very likely he knew, that Ballantine was on the verge of financial ruin, and contemplating flight. He would therefore be in a particularly nervous state. James meets Ballantine after the interview, is told of the incident, expresses his sympathy, and then says: 'My poor fellow, your life is in danger if you go home. Come to my place for the night and you will be safe enough', Ballantine falls into the trap, goes to Daylesford Gardens, and there meets Fanshawe—and his death. How does that strike you?"

Frant rubbed his hands appreciatively.

"Magnificent!" he said. "That's just how it would have happened! I'm sure that's just how it did happen!"

"Quite," rejoined Mallett drily, "and how do we set about proving it?"

"There's only one way to do that," replied Frant, "and that's to find James."

144

Mallett smacked his desk in irritation.

"James, James, James!" he cried. "The crux of this whole case, and not a shred of evidence about him, except that his name is not James, that he hasn't got a beard, and is probably as thin as a rake!"

"You can add another probability to that," remarked Frant, "and that is that he is probably still in France."

"True. We haven't any proof whatsoever that he came back, although we know that his accomplice did, supposing our theory to be true. Well, there it is, Frant. We can only waste time discussing it further, until we get some fresh facts, which may or may not fit into the theory. Now about that question we were discussing this morning, I think I shall get on to the Sussex police and see if they can help us."

At that moment the house telephone rang. The inspector answered it. "Send him up," he said into the instrument.

"The Chief Constable of Dover," he said to Frant. "Now what on earth can he have to tell us?"

The head of the Dover police was an old friend of Mallett, who had collaborated with him more than once before. The inspector knew him for a capable, business-like officer who was not likely to waste his time on trivialities. He came briskly into the room, shook hands with Mallett, nodded to the sergeant and came to business at once.

"Had to come up to see the Commissioner this afternoon," he said briefly, "and thought I might as well bring this with me. Safer than the post, anyway."

He put a sealed packet into Mallett's hands. Mallett opened it and drew out a limp, discoloured blue booklet. He examined it in silence, his eyebrows raised in astonishment. Then he uttered a long whistle.

"Where on earth did you get this?" he asked.

"Fisherman brought it in this morning. Found it just below high-water mark a hundred yards or so east of the harbour last night. Tide sets that way, y'know. Got his statement for what it's worth"—he pulled a folded sheet of official paper from his pocket—"but nothing in it beyond that. May have been in the water days, a week perhaps, impossible to say. High tides all this week and a sou'-westerly gale to help 'em along."

"I'm very much obliged to you," said the inspector. "This may be really valuable. You'll stay for a cup of tea, won't you?"

The Chief Constable shook his head. "Got to be getting along," he said. "Hope it'll help you a bit. You've got a sticky job, I'm afraid. So long."

As the door closed behind him, Mallett tossed the object in his hand to the impatient Frant.

"Exhibit No. 1!" he exclaimed. "What do you think of it?"

Frant looked at it. "A passport?" he said. Then, opening its discoloured cover: "Colin James's passport!"

"No less," said the inspector. "The identical one that our friend of this morning had stolen from him three months ago. It's in pretty bad order, but the name is still legible, thank goodness. Now just turn to page seven."

Frant did so.

"The pages have stuck together," he observed, "and the inside here is quite unspoilt by the water."

"Exactly—luckily for us. What do you find there?"

"The stamp of the authorities at Dieppe and the date—13th November."

"Anything else?"

"Yes—there's something here. Boulogne, and a date in August—that must be the real Mr. James's trip."

"Anything else?"

Frant scanned the passport closely.

146

"Nothing else," he announced.

"Nothing else," Mallett repeated meditatively. "Just what does that indicate to you, Frant?"

"That James went to France, as we knew already, and didn't come back—as James."

"Yes."

"He came back under his own name, or at any rate another one, for which he had another passport."

"Of course, he may be a professional passport stealer, for all we know."

"Then," went on Frant, "having no further use for the James identity, he threw the passport overboard just as the boat reached harbour. He may have been afraid of being searched at Dover, and wanted to make sure it shouldn't be found on him."

"In short," said Mallett, "James is in England. His trip to France was nothing but a blind. As soon as it had accomplished its purpose, back he came. But when, Frant, when? As the Chief Constable says, this passport may have been in the water for days—or for a few hours only."

"Perhaps Fanshawe knows the answer," suggested the sergeant.

"But we have no particular reason to think that they crossed together this time. It is a possibility, of course."

"There is another possibility. James may not have returned from France at all, but given his passport to Fanshawe or to some other confederate, with instructions to plant it on us, just to make us think he had come back."

Mallett shook his head.

"No," he said. "If he had done that, then he would have taken care to see that we did find the passport— left it on board, for example, where a steward would be sure to see it. As it is, it was only by the merest chance that it was discovered. I repeat, James is in England. There can be no more unloading responsibility on to the police in Paris. It's up to us to find him." He pulled at his moustache, and then added: "But I shan't feel a bit like doing it if they don't bring me some tea. I'm famishing!"

17

Seeing a Dog About a Man

Saturday, November 21st

"What's all this nonsense about?"

Susan Jenkinson, her delicate tongue poised on the flap of an envelope which she had just addressed, looked up from her writing-table.

"About what, Father?" she asked. "And do come in, instead of glowering in the door like that. There's a horrible draught. I'm sure it will give Gandhi a chill."

Major-General James Jenkinson, C.B., C.I.E. (Rtd.), in spite of his fiery complexion and parade-ground voice, was a well-trained parent. He meekly entered the room and closed the door behind him.

"I can't think what you wanted to give that dog such an imbecile name for," he complained, pointing to a nondescript mongrel which was dozing in front of the fire.

"It does sound a bit silly now that he's all shaggy," admitted his daughter. "But he was so dreadfully bare and naked at first, it seemed the only name for the poor darling. And it's a good name to shout, too. I'll try calling him Winston, if you really insist, but I don't think he'd answer to it."

The general made no answer to this suggestion, but contented himself with clearing his throat very loudly and fiercely.

"Well, what is it?" persisted Susan, as he remained silent. "You didn't just come in to complain about poor Gandhi, I suppose?"

"As a matter of fact I have come to talk to you about Ga—about that dog of yours," answered her parent. "He's been getting into trouble."

"Trouble? Gandhi? Father, whatever do you mean?"

"Sheep-killing."

"But that's absurd!" cried Susan, thoroughly aroused. "You know he wouldn't dream of it! He has chased a few old hens now and then just for the fun of it, I admit, but he won't even so much as look at a sheep. How could you think of such a thing?"

"It isn't what I think at all," said the general. "It's what the police think."

"D'you mean to say the police are after my poor old Gandhi?"

"I don't know who or what they're after," replied the general testily. "But you know as well as I do that there has been a lot of trouble over sheep-worrying lately on the downs—"

"And nobody's ever dreamt of saying it was Gandhi's fault—"

"—And the police are making enquiries. And I think they are quite right too," he added hastily, before he could be further interrupted.

"But how do you know they are enquiring about Gandhi?" asked Susan.

"That's what I should have told you five minutes ago if you wouldn't keep interrupting. They've just been on the telephone from Lewes."

"Asking about my precious Gandhi?"

"Asking about a large dog belonging to me. I told them I hadn't got a large dog, but that you had."

"Father!"

"Well, that's true, isn't it?" asked the general, instantly on the defensive before the accusing stare of his daughter's blue eyes. "He is your dog, I suppose? You know I've never taken any responsibility for him—no responsibility at all."

"Did you let them accuse Gandhi of worrying sheep and never say a single word for him?" demanded Susan menacingly.

"Certainly not, my dear girl," her father reassured her. "Nothing of the sort. There isn't any accusation. I tell you, they are simply making enquiries."

"What sort of enquiries?"

"What sort of enquiries do the police make in a case like this? How should I know? They're just—well, enquiring."

"Over the telephone? Making all sorts of horrible accusations—"

"Not accusations."

"Well, insinuations against a poor lamb of a dog they've never even seen?"

"I wish you wouldn't run away with ideas like that," said General Jenkinson plaintively. "They do want to see the dog—that's just the point. A sergeant or somebody is on his way now to—well, to make enquiries, as I said."

"And what are you going to tell him when he comes?" asked Susan.

"I'm not going to see him at all," answered the general hastily. "I'm going out to the stables. He's your dog, and you had much better deal with the matter yourself. I take no responsibility—no responsibility at all."

Covering his retreat with his favourite catch-phrase when faced with a difficulty, the general cleared his throat in his most military manner, strode from the room and—since he was a man of his word—did in fact go to the stables, where he devoted a peaceful hour to the contemplation of animals which, whatever their faults, had never numbered sheep-killing among them.

Left to herself, Susan sat in silence for a while. Then she pulled Gandhi's ears lovingly.

"It's all a mistake, isn't it, old boy?" she murmured.

Then she went upstairs to powder her nose. "If it's that nice Sergeant Littleboy who came up when we had the burglary, I know it will be all right," she murmured to herself. "But it's best to take no chances."

It was not the nice Sergeant Littleboy whom, some twenty minutes later, a nervous parlourmaid ushered into the morning-room. Instead, Susan found herself confronting a face which, though she could have sworn it was wholly unknown to her, nevertheless seemed to strike some vague association in her memory. She frowned involuntarily in the effort to identify it, and then, hastily remembering her good manners, assumed her most beguiling smile, and asked the sergeant to sit down.

The new-comer took a chair and as he did so Susan noticed with amusement that his uniform seemed a good deal too tight for him. His chest strained at the buttons of his tunic, and his breath came somewhat short, as though it were impeded by the neck-band. She longed to tell him to undo it, but feared to ruffle his dignity. "I expect he got a bit warm bicycling up from Lewes," she thought, for her windows overlooked the drive and she had seen his arrival.

While these thoughts flitted through his mistress's head, Gandhi conducted his own inspection. Rising in leisurely fashion to his long, ungainly legs, he submitted the stranger to a lengthy, searching sniff. It was some time before he was satisfied. The scent of the uniform trousers vaguely displeased him. Something about it grated on his canine consciousness. But presently he was reassured. Whatever the clothes, the man inside was all right. Quite unmistakably, his instinct passed him as a friend. With an almost imperceptible wag of the tail, he sauntered back to the hearthrug and lay down again, at peace with the world. Susan breathed a sigh of relief. The first crisis was safely over.

She caught the sergeant's eye, and found that he was smiling. Involuntarily she smiled too. Absurdly enough the dog which was the cause of all the trouble seemed to have made them friends already.

"Is that the animal, Miss?" he asked.

"Yes, that's Gandhi. Isn't he rather sweet?" said Susan in her most appealing manner.

"He *looks* harmless enough," was the guarded reply. Then, drawing some papers with an effort from the pocket of his close-fitting tunic, he went on: "I am sure, Miss, that to your mind it seems ridiculous that your dog could possibly be guilty of anything so dreadful as sheep-killing. But it is a serious matter, as you should know very well, living in a sheep-farming country, and we must consider this seriously. If it goes on, we shall have all the shepherds out with guns to protect their flocks, and it will end with the wrong animal killed as like as not. Now I have here some particulars of sheep-killing in this neighbourhood during the last few days. If you can account for your dog's movements during the times in question, we can pass the word on, and he'll be safe. I expect he's pretty well known in this part of the world."

Susan nodded, impressed in spite of herself.

"I'll do my best," she said.

"I'm sure you will, and you won't mind my saying

that it will be all to your advantage if you can supply the names of independent witnesses who can support your statements. We have to be careful in these things, you know."

"Quite."

"Very good. Now the first time is Monday, the 16th of this month, about four p.m."

"Oh, that's an easy one. I had a cold and was indoors. Gandhi was with me."

"I see. Did anyone see him here—besides the people in the house, I mean?"

"Yes, Colonel Follett came to tea, I remember. He knows the dog quite well—he's always making fun of him and his name."

"His address?"

"Rockwell Priory—just the other side of Lewes."

The sergeant noted the name, and went on: "The next day is Thursday last, the 19th. Three in the afternoon."

Susan wrinkled her brow.

"I remember now," she said after a pause. "I went out to the post office that afternoon."

"Was anybody with you?"

"No, but Mrs. Holt at the post office will remember, because Gandhi chased—I mean, her cat ran after Gandhi, all over the shop. There was quite a fuss about it."

The sergeant laughed.

"Excellent!" he said. "I will see Mrs. Holt on my way back. Now there is only one more date—the worst case of all. Friday the 20th, that is, yesterday, some time in the morning."

"I know that can't have been Gandhi," said Susan triumphantly. "I was out riding on the downs that day, and he was with me all the time."

"Are you sure it was Friday morning?"

"Certain. I had been dancing in Brighton the night before."

"How does that help you to remember it?"

"Because the—the person I had been dancing with stayed the night here and we went riding together the next day."

Susan was enraged to feel herself blushing like an early nineteenth-century miss as she made the reply. It may be that the sergeant noticed it, for his next question was: "Is he an independent witness?"

"Not independent exactly," answered Susan, as coolly as she could. "As a matter of fact, we're engaged to be married. If you want his name and address," she went on, "here it is." And she handed him the letter which she had addressed that morning.

"Thank you, miss," said the sergeant. He copied the address in his notebook, and handed back the letter. "May I be allowed to congratulate you?" he added, with grave courtesy.

"Thank you," said Susan in some confusion. First congratulations are sweet, even when they come from a police officer.

Meanwhile the sergeant had risen to his feet.

"Will the wedding be soon?" he asked.

"Oh, quite soon. We've waited long enough as it is."

"Just so. And you'll be living in the country, no doubt?"

"No. We've just had the offer of a share in a farm in Kenya. We shall go out there as soon as we're married."

"Ah, Kenya," said the sergeant musingly. "Well, I hope you'll be very happy there, I'm sure. It's a fine life, they tell me, for those that have a bit of capital behind them."

"Yes, it's a wonderful chance, isn't it?" said the girl eagerly. "It's what I've always wanted, but I never thought we could manage it. I was so surprised when he told me—" She stopped abruptly, as though she had only just realized how far the conversation had led her away from the matter in hand into her private affairs. "Is there anything else I can tell you, sergeant," she went on in a different tone.

"Nothing else, miss, thank you very much," said the sergeant genially, stuffing his papers back into his pocket. "I must be getting back to Lewes now. And I shouldn't worry too much about your dog. Between ourselves I don't expect you will hear any more of this affair. Good morning."

He paused in the doorway. "Perhaps I can post your letter for you in Lewes?" he added.

"Oh, no, thanks. You needn't bother," Susan replied. "I've just thought of something I wanted to add to it, as a matter of fact."

The sergeant gave an understanding smile.

"I see," he said. "Good-bye, then, miss. And good-bye, Gandhi."

General Jenkinson, who had elected to leave the stables just half a minute too soon, encountered the sergeant as he was mounting his bicycle in the drive. He would have passed indoors without noticing him, but he felt that his dignity demanded that he should return the man's salute. As he did so, he looked at him curiously.

"I haven't seen your face before," he said. "You're not a local man, are you?"

"No, sir. I'm temporarily attached to this division."

"H'm," said the general. Then, almost automatically, he found himself exclaiming: "Mind you, I take no responsibility for this dog—no responsibility at all."

"Quite so, sir," said the sergeant soothingly. "The

young lady took full responsibility herself in the matter. But in any case," he went on, "I don't think there is any reason for suspecting the animal. It seems quite clear that he is not the one we're after. I'm only sorry you should have been troubled in the matter."

"No trouble at all," the general assured him, "I'm always only too glad to assist the police in any way. It's part of one's duty as a citizen, in these days especially." He swelled visibly with pride at the assistance he had rendered. "And mind you," he went on, "I shouldn't have been at all sorry if it had turned out to be the dog you wanted. It's a ridiculous dog, and she's given it a ridiculous name. I don't care to have it about the house, I can tell you, sergeant. No pedigree, no manners, and then to hear that name always being shouted about the place— the name of the biggest enemy our Indian Empire has got—it's monstrous!" He paused, and then added: "It isn't even as if it looked like the blighter at all." The circumstance seemed for some reason to add the final drop to his cup of bitterness. He went on: "Of course, she's very fond of the dog, and all that, and I wouldn't see her unhappy if it could be helped, but all the same, I shouldn't be sorry to see the last of it—sheep-killing or no sheep-killing."

The sergeant, who had been making sympathetic noises during this tirade, here took the opportunity to murmur deferentially: "I dare say you will be seeing the last of it before long, sir. I presume the young lady will take it with her when she marries."

"Oh, she told you she was going to get married, did she?" asked the general.

"Yes, sir. But perhaps I oughtn't to have mentioned it."

"God bless my soul, why not? I approve of the affair entirely. She might have done better for herself, I suppose, if she'd wanted to, but Harper is a very decent young fellow—I knew his father well—very decent people—quite a sahib in fact—oh, I approve, absolutely! Though, mind you, the young people nowadays manage these affairs very differently from what they did when I was their age. In those days no young man would go near a girl's parents until he was in a position to keep her. Nowadays they all seem to think they can rush into an engagement without any prospects at all. Then they have to wait, and waiting's a ticklish business for all concerned—unsettles them, if you follow me."

"Quite so, sir," the sergeant agreed. "I've a daughter at home waiting to be married, and I know what it's like."

"You understand, then. Well, it seems to be all fixed up now. Not such a long wait as I feared. They've got round the difficulty somehow—heaven knows how. That's the young people of today again, all over. Secrets, you know. In my young days it was: what's your income, and how do you earn it? Nowadays it's: I can keep your daughter and don't you ask any questions. Still, I suppose we should be satisfied even with that, as things go. We old 'uns aren't treated with the respect we used to get, and that's a fact."

"Quite so, sir," the sergeant said again.

The general looked up, quite surprised to find that he had been addressing a policeman, and not, as he had imagined in the oblivion induced by eloquence, a crony in his club.

"Quite so," he repeated fiercely.

"You'll be sorry to lose her, sir, no doubt," added the sergeant. "I understand they are to live out of England."

"The young fellow means to go out to Kenya, he tells me," said the general. "Got the offer of a partnership in a farm there. And a very good life for a young man—I

158

don't approve of them hanging about in the old country when there's Empire-building to be done elsewhere."

He stopped suddenly, as though conscious that he had been talking a good deal. "Well, I mustn't keep you," he said, nodded curtly and strode into the house.

The sergeant saluted his retreating back, mounted his bicycle and rode slowly away. Before he had gone far, a curve in the drive hid the house from view. Here he dismounted and with a sigh of relief undid the collar of his tunic.

"Phew! That's better!" he murmured. "Well, thank heaven for the garrulity of generals, anyhow. It was a very long shot," he added to himself as he pedalled away once more, "but I've learned something, anyhow. Marriage—money—Kenya—but where the devil does it all fit in?"

Outside the gates he was overtaken and stopped by a police car. A superintendent got out.

"I don't approve of my sergeants going about the roads dressed in that slovenly manner," he said with mock sternness. Then, with a smile: "You'd better get in, Mallett. I've a man here who will take the bicycle back for you."

"Thanks," was the reply. "I've worn these clothes about as long as is good for them."

In the car, the superintendent observed: "By the way, we've found the dog that's been doing the damage."

"Good," said Mallett. "You might let Miss Jenkinson know. I shouldn't like her to be worried unnecessarily."

He could not but feel a hypocrite as he said it.

In the house, Susan was finishing a long postscript to her letter.

"Darling," she wrote, "since I finished this, rather an odd thing has happened. I've had a policeman here—a sergeant, asking questions about Gandhi!—sheep-killing, of all things, as if the poor lamb would even so much as give a sniff at a loathsome great sheep. Of course I told him it was all nonsense, and then he started asking me about dates and things, and one of them was Friday. So, of course, I told him about our heavenly ride on the Downs that day, and how Gandhi was with us every minute of the time, and then—darling, you'll think me a perfect idiot—but he asked me who you were and whether you could back up Gandhi's alibi or whatever you call it, and then before I knew what I was doing I started telling him all about you and how we found we could get married ages sooner than we thought we could and—oh, angel! I do feel such a complete worm to have gone and talked about our private selves to a great red-faced policeman! As if it mattered to a soul except just us! Do forgive me for being such an absolute fool. I feel so beastly about it because, you see, I must tell you now, I have been a bit worried in my mind ever since you told me about the money. It is marvellous having it and all that it means, but, darling, why are you so *mysterious* about it? Honestly, it makes me frightened sometimes. I hate to feel there's something about you I'm not supposed to know. And then when a great fat sergeant starts asking questions about you—he wasn't a bit like an ordinary sergeant, really, much more polite and educated—I suppose that's why I talked to him so much more than I meant. Dearest, do tell me, really, is there anything about this money which—you know what I mean, which the police oughtn't to know about? I don't mind what it is—honestly, I don't—it's only you I care about. Do write soon, if it's only to tell me I'm a nervous little fool. I get these silly frights simply because I love you so much. . . ."

The rest of the letter is irrelevant.

"That sergeant talked a lot," remarked the general at dinner. "I hate a talkative man." He took a spoonful of soup. "Now where all these politicians go wrong about India. . . ."

India lasted well into the savoury.

18

Evidence in Mount Street

Sunday, November 22nd

A flurry of rain, driven on a gust of cold wind, sent pedestrians running for shelter as Mallett turned into Mount Street. It was not a morning for loitering out of doors any longer than was necessary, but the inspector paused a moment beside a street hawker who stood, chilled and dripping, on the pavement. He threw sixpence into his tray, took a box of matches and looked into the man's face as he did so, raising his eyebrows in enquiry.

"Du Pine went in half an hour ago," murmured the hawker.

"Alone?"

The man nodded, and then whined: "Thank you, sir, God bless you, sir," as someone brushed past them.

Mallett put the matches in his pocket and crossed the deserted street. The house he sought was almost immediately opposite, and an observer might have thought it strange that only when he had reached the other side and was within a yard or two of the door did he unfurl the umbrella in his hand. With what seemed unnecessary disregard for any other passers-by, he held it right in front of his face. At that moment two men emerged from the house door. They paused for an instant, looking right and left, before getting into a small two-seater car which was drawn up by the kerb. Not for the first time Mallett thanked the unknown inventor of the umbrella, who has supplied us with a mask, effective and opaque, which can be assumed in a moment, on at least nine days out of ten in an English winter, without attracting the least suspicion. Only one thing was needed to make it perfect from a detective's point of view—an artistically contrived slit in the silk. Mrs. Mallett could never understand why her husband consistently refused to have his umbrella re-covered.

"Du Pine and—who?" the inspector asked himself, as he let down his umbrella in the hall, while the noise of the car receded down the street. "Thin, sandy, not too well dressed, toothbrush moustache—Captain Eales, I should imagine. Better make a note of the number of the car, anyway—VX 7810."

To Mallett, making a note of a fact or name was merely to repeat it once to himself under his breath. Thereafter it was more securely recorded than if it had been copied into a dozen notebooks.

He turned to the porter. "Is Mrs. Eales in?" he asked.

The man nodded. "Oh, she's in all right," he said. There was something of a sneer in his voice, a knowing contempt that to Mallett as a man was intensely disagreeable; for Mallett the detective, like anything else out of the ordinary, it had its interest.

"Then take me up in the lift, please," he said sharply.

"Very good, sir. It's on the second floor. This way."

The maid who opened the flat door to Mallett's ring was young and pretty, but her looks were marred by the expression, a compound of peevishness and indifference, that is to be found on the faces of servants in certain circumstances and in those circumstances only.

"She's under notice," was the inspector's instant reaction. "And she's worried about it, too. Now what is her worry—her next place, or this week's wages?"

"Mrs. Eales?" he asked.

"I don't know whether she can see you, I'm sure," said the maid. "She isn't hardly up yet. Is she expecting you?"

"I'm from Scotland Yard," said Mallett.

"Oh . . ." A gleam of interest appeared in her eyes. Then she shrugged her shoulders. "I suppose you'd best come in then," she added with an instant resumption of her pose of unconcern.

With a swish of her skirt that said as plainly as words: "If she has nasty policemen coming after her, it's no affair of mine, thank goodness!" she led the way to what was evidently the drawing room.

"I'll tell her you're here," she said, in a tone from which the inspector could guess the relish with which she would announce his identity, and left him.

After the cold cheerlessness of the street, the warmth of Mrs. Eales's drawing-room was agreeable. It was indeed a warmth that in a very few moments began to produce on Mallett an impression of stuffiness. Somewhere or other, concealed hot-water pipes were trying to dispel the rigours of the outside world and succeeding, he felt, only too well. The windows were closed, and heavy looped curtains shut out so much of the scanty daylight that he would hardly have been able to examine his surroundings without the aid of the electric light which the maid had turned on before she left him.

"H'm," he said to himself, as he looked around him. "This place would look better by night than by day, I fancy."

It was a fair-sized room, but the multiplicity of objects in it made it look smaller than in fact it was. The modern craze for blank spaces and clean, spare lines had evidently not affected Mrs. Eales. Nothing was here that was not rounded, soft, stuffed, tasselled, fringed. The carpet which covered the floor from wall to wall was thicker and heavier than any carpet had a right to be, the huge divan was piled with cushions of monstrous size. Everything in the apartment breathed an air of expensive and unsophisticated comfort. From a little heap of illustrated society papers on a side-table it might be deduced that its inhabitant had at some time learned to read.

Mallett sniffed. "No books, of course," he murmured. "That's characteristic. And"—he glanced round the walls, "no pictures either. Not so characteristic. I wonder why . . . ."

He looked more closely. On either side of the mirror over the mantelpiece a faint patch of wallpaper showed darker than the rest. Above, two picture-hangers still depended from the rail. Mallett's mind went back to the insolent porter, to the maid under notice. All pointed in the same direction—Mrs. Eales was hard up, sufficiently so to be selling things.

Had anything else gone? he wondered. It hardly seemed possible that a room so crowded could ever have held anything more, but a very short search proved that such was the case. The disinterested maid had evidently neglected her duties for some days and the array of miscellaneous curios and misnamed objets d'art that encumbered the mantelpiece and occasional tables was thinly coated with dust. And here and there a little ring of comparatively clean surface gave evidence that not long since the ranks had been thinned. Mallett counted half a dozen of them without difficulty—silent evidence that here a statuette of jade or ivory, there a china figurine had been sacrified to necessity.

"I *do* apologize for keeping you waiting like this," said a voice behind him. He turned round as Mrs. Eales, a tremulous smile playing on her lips, came towards him with outstretched hand.

"You've come about poor dear Pompey, of course?" she began.

"Pompey?" The inspector was nonplussed for a moment.

"How stupid of me—Mr. Ballantine, I mean. Pompey was just a little pet name I had for him. Silly, of course, these pet names always are, don't you think, Mr.—er—"

"Mallett."

"Mallett—thanks so much—but he used to get so pompous sometimes that it seemed to suit him. And now he's—" she pressed a handkerchief to her lips— "Oh, dear! I can't trust myself to talk about that."

"All the same, madam, I'm afraid I must ask you to talk about it," said Mallett. "I am enquiring into Mr. Ballantine's death, and I am here to find out what light you can throw on it."

"Of course, yes. I must be very brave. Though I don't know what light you will get from poor little me. Do ask me anything you like. Let's sit down here, shall we, and make ourselves comfortable?"

She sat down on the divan, and patted the place by her side in invitation. Mallett had no objection to taking his place beside her. He was not the type of man who would allow his judgment to be affected by propinquity to an attractive woman, even when her charms were reinforced by an exotic scent and a carefully indiscreet display of a silk stocking. What was more important from his point of view, Mrs. Eales had so placed herself that the light of the shaded lamp by the divan shone on her. Sitting himself in semi-obscurity, Mallett studied her with interest.

Like her drawing-room, Mrs. Eales probably looked best by artificial light. Daylight, one felt, would have been too unkind to the lines of anxiety and nervousness about the corners of her eyes and mouth, revealed too clearly that her slender neck and throat were already just a touch too stringy. But seen as Mallett saw her at this moment, she was undeniably a handsome woman. She was dressed in unrelieved black, which set off her fair skin admirably. Her make-up was sufficiently careful to excuse the length of time for which she had kept the inspector waiting. He speculated on what her age might be, but soon abandoned the attempt and found himself watching instead the fascinating play of her expressive brown eyes and thin white hands, neither of which seemed able to be at rest for an instant.

"Will you smoke?" said Mrs. Eales, opening a box of gold-tipped cigarettes. "Oh, but you prefer your own, I expect. Men always do, don't they? I'll have one if you don't mind. Now then, Mr. Mallett, you want to hear all about poor Pompey, I suppose. Of course, this has all been the most frightful shock to me, and I can tell you here and now that I have absolutely no idea how it can have happened. It's—it's been pretty hard, coming just now, you know," she added, and for the first time through the hard brightness of her voice crept a note of sincerity.

"I may take it that Mr. Ballantine's death has affected you rather badly, financially," said Mallett.

She nodded. "The rent of this flat is paid for up to the end of the year," she said, "and after that—well, it's going to be pretty difficult, that's all. Pompey always said he'd put me down for something handsome in his will, but I don't suppose there's anything to leave to anyone now, is there? Still . . . I'm afraid this isn't much use to you, is it, Mr. Mallett?"

"In cases of this kind," answered the inspector gravely, "it is always important to know who stands to profit by the murder. What you tell me is of importance from the point of view of—elimination, shall we say?"

"Meaning that I—? Yes, I suppose I might have guessed that when a man is murdered, his mistress naturally comes under suspicion"—she pronounced the ugly word in a defiant tone—"but in this case, if ever a woman stood to lose by it, I did."

There was a pause, and then Mallett said: "Suppose you were to tell me everything there is to tell about yourself and Mr. Ballantine?"

She shrugged her shoulders. "There's awfully little to tell really," she replied. "We'd known each other off and on for some time—my husband was connected with the turf in those days, and we used to meet at race meetings a good deal. In the end, about two years ago, he took this flat and—there you are."

"And since then he has lived with you here?"

"Yes. Perhaps that's putting it too definitely, though. He might be here for weeks on end, perhaps, and then unaccountably he'd disappear for a bit. Then one day he'd ring up and ask me to meet him for dinner somewhere and afterwards he'd come back here and stay perhaps for a night, perhaps for another long spell. He was an unexpected man in lots of ways. I don't know where he went between whiles. This was his headquarters, though, and of course it was always ready for him whenever he cared to use it."

The phrase woke an echo in Mallett's mind. Where had he heard something very like that before? Of course, Mrs. Ballantine had used almost the same words in her evidence at the inquest. Mount Street and Belgrave

Square had both been open to Ballantine, but he had elected to die in Daylesford Gardens! The reflection prompted his next question.

"Did he ever mention Daylesford Gardens to you— or Colin James?"

"Never. I'm positive of that. As a matter of fact, he didn't discuss outside matters very much."

"You never tried to find out where he went to 'between whiles', as you put it?"

"No. I could guess sometimes, of course. He was always a bit polygamous, was Pompey. I never expected to have him all to myself. I know that sounds rather cattish, Mr. Mallett, but I don't mean to be unkind. He was just made that way. He was an awfully good sort in so many ways, really, you know. People didn't understand him, and he had an iceberg for a wife, but he'd do anything for anyone who knew how to be kind to him." She sighed, and then, turning her lustrous eyes on the inspector, said vehemently: "I'm sure there's a woman at the bottom of this! What else should he have gone to a dreadful little place like that for?"

"There is no evidence of the presence of any woman in the house at Daylesford Gardens," Mallett reminded her. "But there is evidence that he may have been meditating leaving the country about the time that he was killed. What would you say to that, Mrs. Eales?"

She flushed, drew herself up and shook her head. "No, that's not possible," she muttered. "He wouldn't have done that without telling me. After all, I was the person who counted most in his life, however many others there were. Mr. Mallett," she went on, her voice rising as she spoke, "you're not going to make me believe that Pompey meant to leave me in the lurch. I was his, I tell you, his! We made no bones about it—it was a perfectly open affair. Everybody knew we belonged to each other!"

"Including your husband?" Mallett enquired drily.

Checked suddenly in the full flood of her eloquence, Mrs. Eales was silent for a moment, while her flushed cheeks slowly paled.

"Oh, Charles!" she said at last, in a tone that might have meant anything. Then she gave a forced laugh. "Well, yes—including him too, I suppose. Does it matter very much? I mean, you don't want to hear about all the details of a marriage that's—that's been a pretty bad failure, do you, Mr. Mallett?"

The plea for sympathy was prettily contrived, but the inspector ignored it.

"Obviously, I must know anything there is to know about the relations between your husband and Mr. Ballantine," he said.

"But there weren't any—naturally!"

"Am I to understand that you were entirely separated from your husband during your association with Mr. Ballantine?"

Mrs. Eales obviously found some difficulty in answering the question. For the first time in the interview a trace of fear showed itself in her wide-open eyes. Before she could answer, Mallett helped her out.

"You see," he said gently, "we know that already, within a fortnight of Mr. Ballantine's death, you are seeing him again. It hardly looks as if there has been any final breach between you, does it?"

The well-timed disclosure had its effect. Mrs. Eales, he felt certain, had been on the brink of lying, though for what purpose he was still uncertain. Once committed to a falsehood, she would have gone stumbling on from one untruth to another, and her value as a contributor to the story which he was trying to piece together would have gone for good. Now the tension was relaxed and she began to speak again fluently and naturally, though the hint of fear remained to trouble the even tones of her voice.

"No," she said. "There wasn't any final breach. I'm afraid it's a little difficult to put it into words. Our marriage had pretty well broken up by the time I met Pompey, of course, or all this would never have happened. But what had really broken it up was simply money—having no money, I mean, of course. I'm afraid that sounds rather brutal, but it is the fact. We are—we were always quite fond of each other, though it hadn't been a love match by any means. But we were neither of us much good at economizing, and I"—she glanced round the room and settled herself back more deeply among the cushions—"I like my little comforts, you see; I wasn't made to live on bread and cheese and kisses, and when the cash ran short, well—life simply became a cat and dog fight. So when this chance came along I told Charles that I'd simply got to take it. It *was* a bit hard on him, I know, but he saw my point."

"Do you mind if I smoke a pipe?" the inspector asked irrelevantly.

"Oh, not a bit. Please do. I *like* to see a man smoke a pipe." Mrs. Eales's mind reacted to certain stimuli with the infallibility of a penny-in-the-slot machine. In response to Mallett's request the appropriate cliché popped out almost of its own volition.

Behind the comforting cloud of tobacco smoke Mallett tried to visualize the situation Mrs. Eales had been describing—the selfish, shiftless couple, tied in matrimony the bands of which grew more and more frayed as their money melted away, the wife calmly announcing that she was going to live with a man who could keep her in comfort, and the husband—what had his attitude been? What would the attitude of such a man as Captain Eales be?

171

"What terms did your husband make for consenting to this arrangement?" he asked.

"Terms? I don't understand."

"But, Mrs. Eales," said Mallett in tones of gentle expostulation, "you can't really ask me to believe that your husband simply let this happen without trying to get something out of it for himself."

She shook her head.

"I'm afraid Charles made very little out of it," she said. "Mr Mallett, you've simply no idea how hateful it is for me to be talking in this way about my husband, but it was such a *very* difficult position for both of us, wasn't it? I am sure that you, in your profession, learn to look on these things in such a much more broad-minded way than other people would—Well, I promised Charles I'd do what I could for him, and I did try to help him in lots of ways, but there was so little I *could* do. I never had any money to speak of to give him. Pompey was very generous in a way, but he always wanted to know where the money had gone to, and it was really *most* difficult for me. And for Charles, too, of course. Poor fellow, what could he do?"

"He could have divorced you, of course, and got enormous damages from any jury," said Mallett impatiently.

He looked at Mrs. Eales as he spoke, and something in her expression prompted him to add: "Or couldn't he?"

"No, Mr. Mallett," she answered in a voice that was hardly more than a whisper. "That is just what—he—could—not. Oh!" she went on in a sudden passionate outburst, "I do think our divorce laws are the most horribly unjust things that ever were invented! Simply made to make people unhappy and *force* them to break the law if they're going to look respectable! As if a poor creature like that counted as being alive at all, after all these years in a madhouse! Why doesn't someone *do* something about it, I want to know?"

Mallett heard this rigmarole out with an impassive countenance. When it was over, he said in his most matter-of-fact tone:

"Captain Eales couldn't divorce you because he was married already?"

"Yes."

"His first wife being in a lunatic asylum?"

"Yes."

"So that your marriage to him was invalid and bigamous?"

"Yes—and now I suppose it's all got to come out." She was weeping now—or at all events, going through the motions of weeping with great virtuosity.

"Possibly," said Mallett. "But I am investigating murder, not bigamy. Do you feel strong enough to answer any more questions?"

Mrs. Eales raised her head from the cushions in which she had hidden it and began to powder her nose with great vigour.

"Yes. Please go on," she said. "I'm sorry to have been so silly, but you *do* understand how very, very hard things have been for me, don't you, Mr. Mallett?"

"Quite," said the inspector, feeling as he did so that it was a singularly inadequate answer. "Now," he went on, "I must ask you this: when did you first know that your husband was already married?"

"Not when I married him," she answered quickly. "I swear that!"

"When, then?"

"Oh, quite lately—less than two years ago."

"I see. Then it was after you had come to live with Mr. Ballantine?"

"Yes."

Mallett pursed his lips. He thought he saw light.

"Was it Mr. Ballantine who told you?" he demanded.

She nodded. "I believe he'd known about it all along," she muttered half to herself.

"And I suppose," the inspector pursued, "he told you about it when your—when Captain Eales began to threaten divorce proceedings?"

She did not answer. Mallett had no need to press for a reply. The situation was quite clear to him now. Obviously the couple had marked down Ballantine as their prey from the start. Eales had allowed or encouraged his "wife" to ensnare the financier, with the intention, from the first, of making him pay dearly for his pleasure. But Ballantine had been too clever for him. A man in his position would have ample means of investigating the history of anyone he pleased, and when the blackmailing demands began he calmly called the bluff, and threatened the would-be petitioner with exposure as a bigamist. It was a trick quite in keeping with all that he, Mallett, had heard of Ballantine's character. Only one point remained obscure. Was Mrs. Eales telling the truth when she declared her ignorance of her husband's first marriage? If so, perhaps she was as much the victim of his plot as Ballantine had been intended to be. In the upshot, she had chosen to stay with Ballantine, enjoying all the comforts he could provide, while Eales was left out in the cold, an outwitted, impoverished, furiously angry man—a man with murder in his heart, perhaps. "But why wait two years?" Mallett asked himself, and could find, at the moment, no answer.

He turned to Mrs. Eales again.

"In spite of this disclosure, you went on helping your husband as far as you could?" he asked.

She nodded. "He *was* my husband, you see. I couldn't let an accident like that make any difference, could I?"

Mallett with difficulty suppressed a smile. The *naïveté* of the reply was disarming. He went on:

"And what exactly has your husband been doing during these two years?"

She shrugged her shoulders. "I never knew exactly," she said lightly. "He used to sell things on commission a good deal, I think. He tried the motor trade for a time, I know. Then it was silk stockings—anything that offered. He was always dreadfully hard up."

"Where was he living?"

"Oh . . . different places, I suppose."

"Including this one—when Mr. Ballantine was away?"

"No. He'd only come here during the daytime when he knew Pompey would be out. It was a little difficult, of course. Very often we'd have a meal together, and if he had any work to do he could do it here."

The inspector looked round the room. "Here?" he asked.

"In Pompey's study, I mean."

"But since Mr. Ballantine's death, he has been living in this flat, has he not?"

"Oh, yes," answered Mrs. Eales brightly. "But of course that's different, isn't it?"

Mallett expressed no opinion. Mrs. Eales' ideas of propriety were altogether beyond him, and he was thankful that an investigation into them was not within his province. Instead, he rose and said: "Will you show me the study, please?"

"I'm afraid there's nothing much to see here," said Mrs. Eales. "Pompey never kept any private papers here. He used to bring back papers and things from the office to work on them, but he always took them away next morning."

They were standing in the study, a small, sparsely furnished room, which was in marked contrast to the one they had just quitted. An open desk was innocent of papers, except for a few clean sheets of writing-paper. Some of these, the inspector noticed, bore the address of the flat, others the headings of the various companies with which Ballantine had been associated.

"Of course, I never knew what work he did," Mrs. Eales went on. "He kept everything in a big attaché case, and that was always locked."

Mallett forbore to ask how she came to know this. Evidently Ballantine had taken no chances with the lady of his choice.

"I see there is a typewriter over there," he remarked. "Did Mr. Ballantine use that?"

"Yes."

"Captain Eales, too?"

"Sometimes."

"May I use it now?" He eyed her narrowly as he spoke.

"Yes, of course," she replied, obviously surprised at his request.

Mallett took a sheet of the notepaper which bore the name of the London and Imperial Estates Company, and painfully, for he was no expert at the craft, hammered out from memory a replica of the letter which had sent him on his journey to Brighton.

"Thank you," he said when he had done. "I have only a few more questions to ask you. When did you last see Mr. Ballantine?"

"A few days before—before he was found."

"Can't you be more definite? What day of the week was it, do you remember?"

"A Tuesday or Wednesday. I think—Wednesday, I'm almost sure."

"We know that he was alive on the Thursday and Friday of that week. You didn't see him on either of those days?"

"No—I had seen very little of him all that month."

"Or hear from him?"

"No."

"Thank you. Now would you mind telling me, please, what Mr. Du Pine was doing here this morning?"

"Mr. Du Pine?"

"That was what I said."

"I—I really don't know." Her voice faltered. "He came to see my husband. They went away together."

"I know that," said Mallett sternly. "But that isn't an answer to my question. What were they doing together?"

"I don't know," she repeated in a despairing tone. "Honestly I don't. I—I wish I did. He never would tell me."

"You do know, at any rate, that Captain Eales has been in some sort of connection with Mr. Du Pine, then?"

"Yes."

"For how long?"

"Oh, several months, I should think—since last summer, anyway."

"You didn't mention it just now, when I was asking you," Mallett reminded her.

"No—I'm sorry—I didn't think it mattered," was the lame reply.

"But it was some sort of business connection, apparently."

"Yes—but it's no good asking me what it was, because I simply can't tell you. He was always frightfully mysterious about it. It—it rather frightened me."

"What was there to be frightened about?"

She shuddered slightly. "Du Pine," she muttered. "There's something horrible about him. He frightens me badly."

A few minutes later, Mallett took his leave, his mind stored with fresh facts and impressions, and a slip of typed paper in his pocket. Further questioning had wholly failed to elicit anything more from Mrs. Eales as to the nature of her husband's business with Du Pine and the way in which she protested her ignorance convinced the detective that she was being sincere. Only one thing he was able to discover—that the business, whatever it was, had involved some kind of travelling abroad, but whither or when the journeys had been made she could not, or would not, say.

Mallett let himself out of the little study into the passage which led to the front door. As he did so, a flutter of skirts round the corner told him that the sulky maidservant had not been altogether so incurious in her mistress's affairs as she had appeared. He caught up with her in the hall. "You were listening at the door, I suppose?" he said quietly.

"Yes," she answered defiantly. "And what's more, I can tell you something."

"Well?"

"I know when the captain went abroad—and so does *she*, no matter what she says."

"Never mind about your mistress. How do you know?"

"I heard him say it—same as I heard you just now— see? 'I'm making a little trip abroad tonight,' he said, plain as I'm saying it now."

"When was that?"

"In the morning, when he'd come in to see her."

"But what morning?" asked Mallett, exasperated.

"Friday the 13th," answered the maid with gloomy conviction. "You don't forget a date like that in a hurry. And as for starting a journey—I could have told him it would come to no good."

Mallett's face showed no trace of emotion, and the girl, looking eagerly to see the effect of her disclosure, was plainly disappointed.

"It's true, what I'm telling you!" she insisted.

By way of reply, the inspector merely said: "What is your name?"

"Dawes—Florence Dawes, I am, and I—"

"Your evidence may be wanted by us. Where can you be found?"

"Not here, I can't—not after the end of this week, I can tell you that!" she spat out angrily.

Still impassive, Mallett took down the address she gave him and found his way out into the wet and windy street.

"If Mrs. Eales had sold a few more things to pay her servant's wages," he murmured to himself as he strode along the streaming pavement, "she would have saved herself and her husband a lot of trouble."

19

Results of a Little
Quiet Thinking

"That's the machine, all right," said Frant.

Mallett and he stood at a table looking down at two typewritten letters on the office paper of the London and Imperial Estates Ltd. The inspector took a magnifying glass and pored for some time over the documents.

"Yes," he said at last, straightening himself. "This letter," he pointed to the one signed by Lord Henry Gaveston, "was typed by the machine I handled this morning. Do you notice that 'c' a little out of alignment? And if you look through the glass you will see a tiny fault in the crossbar of the capital ' J.' We'll get an expert to check it, but that's good enough for our purposes."

Frant was beaming. He rubbed his hands and twittered with excitement.

"By Jove, we've got him!" he exclaimed. Then he looked up into his superior's face. What he saw there prompted him to add more doubtfully: "Haven't we, sir?"

Mallett's forehead was furrowed with thought. He

180

pulled his moustache until it seemed that the hairs must come out by the roots. For some time he stood in silence as though he had not heard the sergeant's exclamation. At last he turned slowly and said in a restrained voice:

"Have we? Let's sit down and think this over quietly."

He seated himself at his desk and drew a piece of paper from a drawer. Frant sat down opposite him, his effervescence suddenly subsiding to an uncomfortable flatness.

"In the first place," said Mallett, unscrewing the cap of his fountain-pen, "who is 'he'?"

"Well, Eales, I suppose," said the sergeant.

"Eales," repeated the inspector gravely. He wrote the name down at the head of the sheet. "Motive?" he went on.

"Money," said Frant promptly. "Money and jealousy—and perhaps the fear of exposure as a bigamist."

Mallett wrote down: "Money, jealousy, exposure" under the heading "Motive."

"Evidence?" was his next question.

"The letter to the bank," was the ready answer.

"You mean that he could have written it," Mallett pointed out.

"Yes—of course, it doesn't go further than that."

"Access to typewriter," wrote Mallett.

"He could have put it among Ballantine's papers and got it taken to the office that way," Frant went on.

"M'm. Could he? Ballantine kept his attaché case well locked, remember—"

"If Mrs. Eales is telling the truth—"

"Agreed. And so far as we know, he never was in the flat at the same time as Ballantine, and Ballantine was never separated from the case. The first proposition doesn't depend only on Mrs. Eales. It's plain common sense. The second does, though, and she may be wrong

181

there." He wrote a few words and then read: "Query, access to Ballantine's papers?"

"He may have had access to Du Pine's papers, too," put in Frant.

"Yes," Mallett admitted. "We know he was on close terms with Du Pine. But there are some difficulties there. First—why should he have typed the letter at his wife's flat and not at Du Pine's house? Second—isn't that theory equally consistent with Du Pine being his accomplice?"

"That is a possibility—yes," Frant agreed, reluctantly.

"It doesn't look quite so simple, when you come to look into it, does it?" the inspector went on. "Now what else have we to put down under 'Evidence'?"

"His trip abroad on the night of the murder."

Mallett noted the point. "Has it occurred to you", he added when he had finished writing, "that this all turns on our theory that Ballantine was killed by Colin James?"

"Of course."

"Then you think that Eales was James—on the evidence of this letter?"

"Not on that only," Frant objected. "Here's a man who for a long time has had no fixed abode. That would give him plenty of opportunity to live in Daylesford Gardens as Colin James for a few weeks without attracting suspicion. Then you have the mysterious journey abroad on the night of the 13th. I agree that he may be able to explain it away. But until he does—and I've a feeling that he won't be able to—I maintain that we've a strong case against him. All the facts fit him in a way they fit nobody else."

While his subordinate was speaking, Mallett jotted down the salient points. Then he said: "There's one fact that doesn't fit him very well, you know."

"What fact?"

"The beard. Eales has a moustache, as I think you know—a reddish toothbrush affair. I know what you're going to say, Frant. He could have covered it up with a false one which would go with the beard. But James—the real James, I mean—had his upper lip clean-shaven. Why go to the trouble of stealing a passport and making yourself up as the man it belongs to, if you won't even take the trouble to shave?"

"Murderers aren't necessarily logical," protested Frant. "It's absurd to be prepared to murder and to boggle at shaving off your moustache, but people do absurd things. I don't find anything impossible in the idea."

"Very well, then. We keep Eales in the running. By the way, how does that square with your theory of yesterday—that the murder was done by James and Fanshawe in collaboration?"

Frant pondered.

"It doesn't," he admitted. "That is, we have no clue as yet to any connection between Eales and Fanshawe—except just this, that they both went abroad on the same night."

"And that is something," the inspector agreed. "It would be asking rather a lot from coincidence to expect that three people mixed up in this case happened to choose the same night to travel. Apart from that, though, there is no connection between them. Moreover there is a connection, and a close one, between Eales and Du Pine, which doesn't seem to square with his having anything to do with Fanshawe, Du Pine's mortal enemy. To all appearances, they are two quite independent people who happen to have reason to hate the same man. At the moment I'm inclined to think that if Eales goes in, Fanshawe comes out."

He wrote a few more words on his paper.

"May be James," he murmured. He underlined the word "may." "It doesn't seem to me to make sense," he complained. "That moustache still bothers me. What you say may be right enough as a general proposition, but it doesn't seem to me to fit this case. James, whoever he was, laid his plans with the greatest care, took every precaution. Why should he omit this obvious and simple one? And then why did Eales tell his wife that he was going to France? It was quite unnecessary. As James, he advertised the fact, naturally. But doesn't it seem to follow that as Eales, he would keep it as dark as possible?"

Frant groaned. "I give it up," he said. "You seem to have an answer to everything. I was a fool to jump to conclusions. We're not an inch farther on than we were."

"Don't let's be in too much of a hurry," said Mallett. "We needn't go to the other extreme all at once. All these objections may be explained away. I'm only saying that at present we haven't the evidence to arrest Eales for murder." He drew out another sheet of paper and went on: "After all, Eales isn't the only pebble on our particular beach. We've got quite a number of facts accumulated here now, pointing different ways, and to different people. I propose that we take each one in turn, and treat him just as we did Eales and see what it amounts to. Who comes next?"

"Du Pine?" suggested the sergeant.

"Yes, he seems to follow logically. Motive?"

"He wanted to get his share of the boodle which he knew Ballantine was making off with."

"Good enough. Evidence?"

"He could have introduced the letter to the bank among Lord Henry's papers."

"Certainly. Anything more?"

"He was doing something shady in association with

184

Eales, so the arguments against Eales apply to him to some extent."

"Yes . . . Du Pine could not have been James, I take it?"

"No. I've checked him up, and he was in London on the Saturday and Sunday following the murder."

"Not James," wrote Mallett. "Must therefore have had assistance."

"That seems to follow," Frant agreed. "The only other point against him I can suggest is his general behaviour."

"It was certainly uncouth enough to frighten Mrs. Eales fairly considerably," said Mallett.

"And he himself is frightened very badly of something."

"To judge from what I saw at the inquest, the something was a someone, and his name was Fanshawe." Mallett finished Du Pine's meagre dossier, and went on: "Fanshawe! I think he deserves a sheet to himself."

"No difficulty about a motive there."

"Motive overwhelming," went on to the paper. Then followed briefly: "Evidence—(a) Threats; (b) Opportunity; (c) Travel."

"That looks fairly impressive," remarked Frant.

"Yes. How much more impressive it would be if we didn't have to add something." And Mallett wrote: "Not Colin James."

"How lucky for Fanshawe," he observed, "that James and Ballantine were seen going into Daylesford Gardens, and James was seen coming out."

"There's no doubt about the bona fides of the witness Roach, is there?" asked Frant.

"None at all. I've had him looked up. He seems to be a most reliable little man. By the way, is there any evidence that Fanshawe has profited by the crime—financially, I mean?"

"No. He is living very quietly with his sister in Daylesford Court Mansions. I should say he was decidedly badly off."

"Did you go to Rawson's in Cornhill to see whether he got his ticket to Paris from there?"

"Yes. It was quite correct and in order."

Mallett sighed and placed the paper neatly on the others.

"Harper comes next, I think," he said. "His motive is the same as Fanshawe's, only at one remove, so to speak, *plus* money, perhaps. And unlike Fanshawe, he has got suddenly richer since the murder. Like Du Pine, he has something to hide, and something frightens him. Unlike Eales or Du Pine, he does not appear to have had any previous connection with Ballantine, or knowledge of his transactions. Unlike anybody else on the list, he professes actually to have seen James—and, incidentally, either accidentally or on purpose, he has contrived to cover James's tracks very thoroughly. An odd person, Harper, and in an odd position too. He seems to link up so many different parts of the puzzle."

"You don't think he did the murder, do you?" said Frant.

"Did it? No . . ."

"Or helped to do it in any way?"

"He certainly helped to do it, by letting James the house in Daylesford Gardens. That may be just coincidence, of course. But if you could have seen him on the day we discovered the body—I tell you, Frant, that boy knows something! The question that's worrying me is—does he know that he knows it?"

There was silence for a space, broken only by the faint scratch of the inspector's pen travelling over the paper.

Another sheet was added to the pile, and then the two men sat without speaking, each absorbed in his thoughts.

"Then there's Crabtree," said Frant at last.

"Crabtree? Yes, of course, the servant. We mustn't forget him. Let's see, his motive is Harper's—at one remove further this time. He was at Daylesford Gardens, and we only have his word for it that he left on Friday morning. He might have stayed there all day and finished Ballantine off when he came in with James."

"That makes him an accomplice of James," said the sergeant.

"Not necessarily, though it looks like it. But James might have left Ballantine behind him alive and well, and then Crabtree took the opportunity to kill him and fill his pockets with whatever cash Ballantine had on him. With some of the money he goes to Spellsborough races, and the rest he gives to Harper who, in return, promises him a good job, in Kenya probably. How does that strike you?"

"Not very favourably, I must say."

Mallett laughed. "Nor does it me," he admitted. "But you see that, given the right assumptions, there's not one of them we can't make a case of sorts against. And we know perfectly well that they're assumptions no jury in the world would be prepared to make. And all the time we're no nearer than we were at the start to answering the two questions we've got to answer before we have the full history of this crime—who was Colin James, and why did Ballantine go to Daylesford Gardens?"

"They're a mixed bag of suspects," said Frant, stirring the little sheaf of papers with his finger.

"Yes, but they're all connected in one way or another. Beginning with James, you have Crabtree who kept house for James, Harper who got the job for Crabtree, Fanshawe who was Harper's father's friend, Du Pine who

187

is afraid of Fanshawe, and Eales who does some dirty work for Du Pine. Add Mrs. Eales to the chain and you bring it back to Ballantine."

"Well, we wanted to find the connection between James and Ballantine," said the sergeant with a grin, "and here it is. But it is a desperately roundabout one."

"Yes, it's rather like the old woman and the pig who wouldn't get over the stile. But we've still got another suspect to put on the list."

"You mean Mrs. Eales?"

"No; though there are still some things about that lady I don't understand. I don't expect any man could understand her altogether, for the matter of that."

"Mrs. Ballantine, then?"

"No, no. This isn't a woman's crime. Besides, she had long got past the stage of hating Ballantine enough to murder him, if I'm any judge of character. I think she was the kind of woman to go on making the poor sinner's life a burden to him with her rectitude and patience, and to take a pride in putting up with all the unhappiness he caused her. The suspect we've got to put on the list is a more dangerous character than that."

"Who do you mean?"

"X," answered the inspector. "The unknown quantity, who may upset all our calculations. It's fatal to forget him. Whenever you make a list of possible criminals, you are apt to put yourself in blinkers and forget that anyone exists outside your list. Always put in X, and keep a sharp lookout for him."

"And how do we set about finding X?" asked Frant, with heavy irony.

"I propose to do a little quiet thinking," said Mallett. "Unless we're unexpectedly lucky, I don't think anything more is going to turn up to help us. The facts are here," he pointed to the desk, "and I've got to spell them out."

"But you said just now," Frant objected, "that there's nothing there to justify a conviction."

"Perhaps not. But when I know where to look, it won't be too hard to find the material I want. At least, I hope not. There is such a thing, of course, as knowing who the murderer is and not being able to bring it home to him."

Frant rose to go.

"While you are doing that," he said, "do you mind if I do a little work on my own?"

"Of course not. What had you in mind?"

"I still think Eales is the likeliest man on our little list. Certainly he's the one we know least about. I should like to apply for a warrant for his arrest."

"A warrant?"

"Yes—for bigamy."

Mallett stared at him. "But you can't," he said. "Not on Mrs. Eales story to me alone."

"I don't mean to. If Ballantine found out about his first marriage, there ought to be some record of it in his papers. Renshaw has them all. I shall ask him to let me go through them."

Mallett was never slow to show appreciation of a subordinate's idea. "That's a really good suggestion," he said. "Do that. Find out if we can prove Mrs. Eales's story to be true, and let me know."

"And then, may I apply for a warrant?"

The inspector smiled, somewhat in the manner of a parent humouring a child anxious for a treat.

"We'll see," he said. "Perhaps when I've thought this out, we shall be wanting a warrant for something more serious than bigamy".

"Then you think I may have been right about Eales after all?"

"No, I don't!" roared the inspector, exasperated. "I

189

don't think anything yet. I'm only asking you to go away and let me think!" And Frant found himself fairly hustled out of the room.

"Thinking seems to be a whole-time occupation for some people," was the sergeant's unspoken comment as he left. "And I'm prepared to bet that the first thing he does is to go out and make a pig of himself over lunch."

Frant did not return for some hours. When at length he again walked along the corridor that led to Mallett's room, it was with the long, impatient strides of a bearer of good news. He knocked at the door, and, receiving no answer, entered at once. The words he was already framing died away in an exclamation of surprise and disgust. His superior officer was lying back in his chair, his eyes closed, his feet miraculously poised on an overturned waste-paper basket which seemed to be on the verge of crumpling beneath their weight, his great body stirring gently and rhythmically with the deep-taken breaths of sleep.

Exactly when Mallett woke up, Frant could not say. He was only gradually aware, as he looked down on him, that he was being scrutinized from under half-closed eyelids, that the corners of the mouth had twisted slightly into a friendly, almost mischievous grin. This stage lasted for a few seconds only, and then, quite suddenly, the whole man started to life at once. With a convulsive jerk the inspector sat up abruptly in his chair, his feet under him, his eyes wide open. The waste-paper basket was sent spinning across the room by the sudden movement until it was brought up short by the opposite wall. There it remained, the sole witness to an unfortunate lapse in the career of an exemplary officer.

It was an embarrassing moment for the sergeant, whose genuine respect for Mallett reinforced the dictates of discipline in constraining him to do his best

190

to look as though nothing unusual had happened. But Mallett remained genially unashamed.

"Do you know," he said with the air of one imparting a deep confidence, "I was almost asleep when you came in? I was tired," he added, somewhat unnecessarily.

The agreeable smile had not left his lips, and this emboldened Frant to ask, with a touch of malice: "Did you have a good lunch?"

"I haven't had any," was the surprising reply. "Is it late?"

"Nearly three o'clock."

"Good lord! Well, it can't be helped. Now tell me what you've been doing."

Frant was so astonished by the inspector's uncharacteristic indifference to his meal-times, which he felt must portend some occurrence of great importance, that the news he had come hot-foot to tell seemed in comparison a minor matter. But as he told his story something of his earlier enthusiasm returned, and the obvious interest with which Mallett listened gave him additional encouragement.

"I went straight to Renshaw after leaving you," he began, "and he gave me a free hand with all Ballantine's papers. There was nothing at all to be found among the private documents that helped me in the least. There were very few private documents of any kind, for the matter of that."

"I'm not surprised," commented Mallett. "For one reason or another, Ballantine took care to leave very little in the way of personal papers behind him."

"Then it occurred to me," Frant went on, "to look at his passbooks. I thought that if he had been investigating Eales's past, he would probably have employed someone to do the donkey-work for him."

"An enquiry agency, you mean?"

"Just so. There aren't so many of them in London, and I carry most of their names in my head. I began with the passbooks of three years ago and it wasn't very long before I came across a series of payments to Elderson."

"Elderson?"

"Yes, the name struck me at once. You remember the clever little man who was in U Division and had to resign from the force over the Barkinshaw affair? He set up in business as a private enquiry agent in Shaftesbury Avenue."

"I remember him perfectly well," said Mallett. "I think we've had some trouble with him since. Wasn't there rather a serious complaint from one of his clients a year or two ago?"

Frant nodded. "The complaint was withdrawn later," he said, "but it gave friend Elderson a bad fright at the time. I thought that fact might come in handy if I had to put pressure on him, and so it turned out."

"You went to see him, then?"

"Straight away. He was very smooth-spoken and ingratiating—just as he always used to be—until I told him what I'd come about. Then he turned difficult at once. He said he was very sorry, but his business being a highly confidential one, he made a point of keeping no record of his clients' business. He showed me his advertisements, in which he guaranteed absolutely that all records were destroyed as soon as a case was concluded. They looked most impressive, I must say." Frant chuckled at the recollection.

"Well?"

"Well, I reminded him of the affair we've just been speaking of, and suggested to him that if he wanted to put himself in a better light with Scotland Yard, perhaps it would be as well if he thought the matter over again."

"Most immoral," grunted the inspector.

"Wasn't it? Well, the long and the short of it was that in the end he admitted, most reluctantly, that in the very peculiar circumstances of this case, he had perhaps allowed a few records of his dealings with Ballantine to survive. I asked to see them, and he went to his safe and brought out the fattest file you ever saw in your life. I should think Ballantine must have been an exceptionally valuable client of his. He seems to have made it his business to pry into the private affairs of every man, woman and child he ever had to deal with."

"Including Eales?"

"Including Eales. Including also Mrs. Eales—the first and second."

"Aha!"

"I've brought the relevant papers away with me," went on Frant with a triumphant air, "and here they are. Here is a copy of Elderson's letter to Ballantine enclosing a certified copy of the certificate of marriage between Charles Roderick Eales, bachelor, and Sarah Evans, spinster, on the 14th July, 1920, at the parish church of Oakenthorpe, Yorkshire; here is his report of his visit to the North Riding County Asylum and a transcript of the register of inmates there; here is the name and address of the doctor who certified her; here is—"

"Stop, stop!" Mallett begged. "I'll take it as read. I'm a tired and hungry man, remember. Eales is a bigamist. We knew that already, but now we know just how, when and where he bigamized. We know when he was lawfully married and who to, and which asylum his wife is in. We have only got to send up to Yorkshire to get the evidence and he can be arrested whenever we like. Is that what you were going to say?"

"Well, yes," the sergeant admitted. "It was—more or less."

"Then there's nothing more to be said—except to congratulate you on a smart piece of work. It was a really brilliant idea to get at the information through Ballantine's passbook. And what do you propose to do next?"

"Exactly what you suggested just now, sir—get the evidence and put Eales under lock and key as soon as possible. When we do, I think we shall find out something further about Master Eales."

"I think we shall," said Mallett meditatively, and was silent for a moment, a barely perceptible smile flickering over his features. "In any case," he added, "I think we can say we have done a useful bit of work today."

It was Frant's turn to smile. After the hard work that he had just completed, Mallett's "we" struck him as decidedly entertaining, to say the least of it. His amusement did not pass unobserved.

"I said 'we'," repeated Mallet. "May I point out that you haven't asked me yet what I have been doing while you were away?"

"But you told me yourself," objected the sergeant. "You have been thinking, haven't you?"

"Exactly—but I thought you might be interested enough to enquire the result of my efforts. Or doesn't thought interest you?"

"Very much indeed," Frant hastened to reassure him.

"I am delighted to hear it. Well, then, after some hard and decidedly tiring thinking"—Mallett stifled an enormous yawn—"I have come to some definite conclusions. One definite conclusion, perhaps it would be more accurate to say, from which the rest follows as a matter of course."

"And that conclusion is—?"

"The identity of Colin James."

Frant took a sharp breath of excitement. The inspector went on calmly: "That identity once established, it becomes perfectly simple to ascertain who killed Ballantine, and why, and how and all the rest of the story."

"Of course, we've always assumed that. But who is James?"

"Unfortunately," Mallett proceeded, "having done that, we are only halfway to our objective. The business of detection", he continued pedantically, "is in two parts. First, we have to discover the criminal. That can be done, as I have done it in this case, by pure deduction from sometimes very slender evidence. Second, we have to prove his guilt to the satisfaction of a jury. That, as you know very well, is often the hardest part of our task. I think that in this instance it won't turn out too impossibly difficult, now that I know exactly what I am looking for. And for a start—"

Frant could bear it no longer. "But James! James" he almost shouted. "Who is Colin James?"

"As I was saying—for a start, I think I shall go and have another chat with Gaveston."

Frant stopped in the act of repeating his question, open-mouthed, while he groped for the significance of the name. "Gaveston?" he said at last. "The silly old man who signed the letter? I don't understand. What earthly good can he be?"

"No, not that one, but his brother, Lord Bernard. A much more interesting person to talk to, altogether. I shall enjoy seeing him again. Last time we met, he dropped something in the course of conversation that makes me think he has some knowledge which will be useful."

The sergeant shrugged his shoulders. "This is all very mysterious," he grumbled. "I'm supposed to be helping you in this case, and you won't tell me the most important thing in it. If you won't, you won't, I suppose, but I don't see why I should be kept in the dark."

Mallett's eyes were dancing mischievously. "Think, Frant, think," he taunted him. "It's not so difficult when you get down to it. We had a list, didn't we? Let's see, now, who were they?"

"Eales, Du Pine, Fanshawe, Harper, Crabtree," said Frant rapidly, "and—"

"Yes?"

"And, of course—X."

"I think we can leave him out now."

His pencil played busily across a writing-pad. Then he tore off the sheet and passed it across the desk.

Frant read as follows:

"Identity of Colin James.

"The following are the names of the chief suspects in the case of Lionel Ballantine:

> Eales
> Du Pine
> Fanshawe
> Harper
> Crabtree."

"Do you mean," he asked, "that James is one of the people on this list?"

"Certainly."

Frant shook his head slowly, as he read once more the list of names he knew so well. Then Mallett's hand reached over towards him and the pencil made a cross against one of them. He stared at it, then looked up again, his face still clouded with perplexity.

"But I don't understand," he muttered. "How—"

"It is a bit difficult at first sight," Mallett admitted, "like most very simple things. Let me see if I can make it a little clearer."

He took the paper back again, and wrote a few further words at the foot.

"Now do you see?" he asked, handing the sheet across once more.

There was a strained silence while the sergeant slowly spelled out the significance of what Mallett had just written. Then his face suddenly cleared, and he burst into a peal of laughter.

"Good Lord!" he exclaimed. "Why didn't we think of that before? It explains everything!"

"Everything?" said Mallett reflectively. "I'm not so sure. The murder—yes. That is after all the essential question. But I am still troubled in my mind about *these* fellows"—his pencil stabbed the page once and again. "How do they fit into the story? I shan't be satisfied until I know. And now would you mind sending out for some sandwiches for me—beef ones, with plenty of mustard? There's a lot to discuss still, and I should hate to die of starvation in the very moment of success."

Frant went to the door, and then turned and picked up the slip of paper.

"In case you don't survive until I get back," he remarked as he pocketed it, "I should like to keep this as a memento."

Mallett leaned back in his chair with a smile. "The last will and testament of John Mallett," he murmured.

He was already asleep by the time the sound of Frant's feet had ceased to echo down the corridor.

20

Lord Bernard Remembers

Tuesday, November 24th

"I'm not sure whether his lordship can see you now, sir," said the butler, doubtfully. "Is it anything very important?"

"Yes," said Mallett. "It is—very important. Just tell him that Inspector Mallett wants to see him, will you? I shan't keep him for more than a few moments."

It was a quarter to eleven in the morning. Outside the door of Lord Bernard Gaveston's elegant little house in Hertford Street the Visconti-Sforza, awaiting her master's pleasure, was undeniable evidence that he had not yet gone out. But the man still seemed to hesitate.

"If you will wait a minute, I will enquire," he said severely.

He grudgingly admitted Mallett into the hall and vanished within. After a very short absence he returned and with an air compounded of resignation and disapproval said: "Come this way, please."

Mallett followed him upstairs and was ushered into a small, square room on the first floor.

"This is the gentleman, your lordship," said the butler.

Lord Bernard was at breakfast. He smiled cheerfully at his visitor and called to the butler:

"Bring another cup for Mr. Mallett, and some more coffee."

Mallett protested, with all the self-conscious rectitude of an early riser, that he had breakfasted several hours ago. Lord Bernard retorted with unanswerable logic, that for that reason he was all the more entitled to take further refreshment in the middle of the morning; and went on, to the profound embarrassment of the butler, to point out that at that moment every member of his grossly overpaid and underworked household was indulging in the orgy known as "elevenses," and if they were entitled to it, how much more a busy detective? The argument, and the delicious scent of coffee wafted to his nose from the breakfast table, were together too much for the inspector, and he capitulated.

"It is an odd thing," said his lordship, when the coffee had been brought, "but though I am not generally considered a particularly hospitable man, whenever I meet you I always seem to be pressing you to eat and drink against your will. Last time it was dinner, I remember."

"It was a very good dinner," said Mallett gratefully.

"Not bad. Let me see, we had a *sole vin blanc* and a *tournedos*—rather overdone, didn't you think? I can't remember the sweet for the moment."

"At all events," said Mallett, "I am extremely glad to find your memory is so good, because I have come here simply to tax your memory on one subject."

Lord Bernard shook his head.

"Don't depend on it, Inspector," he said. "My memory is not on the whole a good one. I remember the things I

199

happen to be interested in, like everybody else, that's all. Leading a rather idle and worthless life as I do, dishes and the vintages of wines bulk rather largely in my mind, I'm afraid. Yours, I expect, is full of details of your cases. I dare say you tend to be quite forgetful outside them, unless you are a superman—which I suppose a detective ought to be. I know musicians who are hopelessly absentminded about ordinary things, but can carry the full score of half a dozen symphonies in their heads. It's a form of specialization."

While he was speaking, Mallett was only attending with half his mind. His eyes meanwhile were travelling round the airy, charmingly furnished room. Something that he had noticed when he entered it had touched a chord of memory—something connected with the matter in hand. What was it? Presently he found it. It was a small, brilliantly executed oil painting of a woman's head, which hung over the mantelpiece. He had seen that face once before, and though the woman in the portrait was some years younger, at least, than the original when he had met her, he had no difficulty in recognizing her. It was Mrs. Ballantine. He had just established the fact to his satisfaction when Lord Bernard's little discourse came to an end.

"Just so," he said. "Everybody's memory works in a different way, and you never can tell what will jog it into action again. What I have come to ask you is about something you said at that dinner, and about something you would have gone on to say if you had not been interrupted."

Lord Bernard gave him a keen look.

"You must play fair with me, Inspector," he said. "Before we go any further, you must tell me whether this in any way implicates my brother. Because if so—"

"I can promise you," replied Mallett, "that nothing

you can tell me will incriminate your brother. Indeed, I can go further and give you my assurance that I am quite convinced that Lord Henry is in no way concerned with this crime."

"Very good. Then go ahead."

"We had finished dinner, and you were talking about Ballantine. You told me that you had always distrusted him, principally because of his clothes. You mentioned that he always gave you the impression of a man dressed up for a part. Then you went on to speak in particular of the last time you saw him at his place in the country, where you had gone with Lord Henry to help his office staff to produce a play. I am speaking from recollection, but that is roughly the line the conversation took."

"There's not much wrong with your memory, is there?" said Lord Bernard with a smile. "I congratulate you. But I'm afraid I'm interrupting. Please go on. What did I say next?"

"That's just the point. You were going to say something and had got so far as 'That reminds me—' when you were interrupted. Now I have reasons for thinking that if you can tell me what you were about to say, it will help me to prove who murdered Ballantine."

"That sounds extremely improbable, if I may say so," Lord Bernard commented.

"It is true, none the less, and I must ask your lordship to take my word for it."

"Obviously, I must. You know your business, and I don't. Well, I'll do my best. Just run over my lines again, and I'll see if I can remember my cue."

Mallett repeated the words again.

"That reminds me—that reminds me—" murmured Lord Bernard to himself. "No, I'm sorry, Inspector, but it doesn't come back. You see, I'm not really remembering that evening at all. I can vaguely recollect using the words you have mentioned, but that is only because you have put them back into my mind, and they sit there, isolated so to speak, and sterile, because the context isn't there. Just cudgelling my brains and trying to remember is no good. If I could only think myself back into the mood of that evening, feel as I did then, perhaps the words would start breeding in my brain and have issue, the issue that was stifled at birth last Thursday night. Though heaven knows, Inspector," he added, "whether it will be any good to you when it does arrive!"

"Do you think you can do that, then?" asked Mallett.

"The mind's a funny thing," said Lord Bernard. "I've noticed sometimes that it helps if you stop concentrating directly on the subject, and shift your attention elsewhere, not on to something different altogether, but a bit to one side, if you follow me. I don't want to waste your time, but if I were to discuss the Ballantine affair quite generally, it might attain your purpose, as well as amusing me. Do you mind doing that?"

"Not at all."

"Very well, then. Have you made any discoveries in the case recently?"

Mallett considered for a moment. Then he got up and walked across the room to get a nearer view of the picture. He noticed, for the first time, that there was an inscription on the frame, some lines of verse which were new to him. He read:

"Who her will conquer ought to be
At least as full of love and wit as she,
Or he shall ne'er gain favour at her hands.
Nay, though he have a pretty store of brains,
Shall only get his labour for his pains,
Unless he offer more than she demands."

He read it through twice before he took the plunge.

"Yes," he said. "I have discovered something of interest since I came into this room."

Lord Bernard was looking at him with an expression of amusement.

"I congratulate you," he said. "Yes, that painting is something of interest, certainly—though, to be frank, I hardly expected you to recognize it as such. It is one of Jules Royon's best works. He would have been a famous man if he had lived. Personally, I don't think there has been a better painter in France since Renoir died. If you like, I can show you some water-colours of his which are little masterpieces, too."

Mallett shook his head.

"I'm not interested in the painting," he said, "but only in the subject."

"The subject? Ah! You recognize her then?"

"I do. And it occurs to me that your interest in Ballantine was perhaps rather closer than you suggested in our talk at Brighton the other evening."

Lord Bernard laughed.

"I'm afraid you're exploring a mare's nest," he said. "Yes, that's Mary Ballantine's portrait all right. But you can see for yourself that it was done some years ago. In point of fact, I have not seen her since her marriage—or, indeed, for some time before that. No, if you're looking for a jealous lover to fix the murder on, I fear you will have to look elsewhere. The picture is here as a work of art, merely."

"And the inscription?" Mallett asked.

"Ah, the inscription! But that just proves my point! When I tell you, Inspector, that it was her own choice! I had commissioned the portrait from Royon because I was—not to put too fine a point on it—in love with her, or as nearly in love as makes no matter. She had it framed and sent to me, with those lines underneath. I never had anything to do with her again." He crossed the room in long strides, and standing in front of the painting, read the lines over softly to himself. "They are beautiful, are they not?" he went on. "Yes, and very proper to be addressed by a despairing lover to his mistress. But when a woman writes them of herself—when she sets herself up on that sort of pedestal—no thank you! 'Unless he offer more than she demands', indeed! What right has any woman to demand that sort of approach from a man? It's the fault of the poets, I suppose, who put such absurd ideas into women's heads, so that they trade on their femininity, but how any woman of sense—"

He stopped abruptly in the heat of his tirade, and his expression changed all at once.

"A woman!" he exclaimed. "There was a woman at Brighton, wasn't there? A girl who looked happy? Inspector, you never told me—what was it exactly that interrupted me in what I was telling you that evening? Can't you remember?"

"I remember perfectly well," answered Mallett. "You were interrupted by your brother, who noticed a pretty girl on the dancing floor below where we were sitting."

"Why on earth didn't you mention it before? Why, it's the crux of the whole case," said Lord Bernard in growing excitement. "I can see it all now. We were in the gallery, watching a terrible lot of old dowagers and their gigolos, when suddenly she appeared. It's as clear as crystal now!"

"Then you do remember?" the inspector asked eagerly.

Lord Bernard was back at the breakfast table, arranging chairs.

"Do you ever go in for reconstructing the crime at

Scotland Yard?" He asked. "I think now that if we reconstruct our dinner-party, whatever was in my mind then ought to come back to it again. I can't promise, but by all the rules it should. Now let me see, you were in the middle, weren't you? And I was *there*, and my brother away on the left. This chair will have to do for him. You will have to double the parts, if you don't mind. Would you care for a cigar to complete the illusion? No? Very well. We have got to imagine that we are in the Riviera Hotel, and the gallery will come just about where the edge of the carpet is. Is that right?"

"Absolutely."

"Good. Now just prompt me to start with, and we will see what happens. How do I begin?"

" 'I always distrusted Ballantine,' " Mallett began. " 'It would be difficult to say why.' "

" 'I think it was his clothes chiefly,' " Lord Bernard chimed in.

" 'Why his clothes?' "

" 'Ballantine's clothes revealed something in his character which I didn't like.' "

" 'Surely a millionaire can wear what he likes?' "

" 'Yes, but why should he be always too well dressed? Or, I should say, over-dressed? He gave me the impression of acting a part?' "

Mallett here assumed Lord Henry's thick voice as best he could.

" 'You didn't see much of him,' " he objected.

" 'Oh, yes I did—at race meetings, especially.' "

" 'Naturally, he dressed up for race meetings,' " went on Mallett-Gaveston.

" 'Ah, but it wasn't only race meetings.' " Lord Bernard began to speak faster and with more and more animation. " 'Do you remember taking me down to his place in the country for the dramatic show his staff was giving?

205

He looked a dreadful sight'—or words to that effect—
'and that reminds me—' "

So convincing was his acting, that Mallett too was carried away by the part he was playing.

" 'By George!' " he said enthusiastically, " 'there's a
real good-looker down there at last!' "

His hand, dramatically extended, pointed, not, as it
should have done according to the rules, downwards,
but directly at the door in front of him. And, as though
in response to a magic incantation, it opened, revealing
the prosaic outlines of the butler.

The latter was of the ambassadorial type whose dignity is not easily perturbed. Only by the slightest lift of
his eyebrows did he recognize that there was anything
irregular in the situation that confronted him. And when
he spoke, it was only to say: "Will your lordship require
the car to wait any longer?"

"Oh, go away, Waters! Go away!" roared the master,
and burst into a fit of laughter.

Mallett, for himself, felt more than a little foolish. He
had been made to look ridiculous and he felt extremely
doubtful whether any good purpose had been served by
it. Meanwhile Lord Bernard, still laughing, pushed back
his chair and rose to his feet.

"The séance is over!" he announced.

Mallett's heart sank.

"Then you still can't remember?" he asked.

"On the contrary, I remember everything. And what
I remember is so perfectly trivial and irrelevant that I
can only apologize for making you waste your time."

"I am the best judge of that," returned the inspector.
"What was it?"

"Simply this—I was going to say: 'That reminds me
that the lamented Ballantine still owes me some money
for that dramatic society of his.' "

"In what way?"

"For the dresses and wigs and so on. As I was in charge, I ordered them all, and then when the bill came in he was to settle it. He hadn't done so up to the time he was killed, and now the wig and dress people are going for me."

"I suppose the members of the dramatic society are really liable to you," suggested Mallett.

"Yes, but how can you ask those poor devils to pay? They've lost their jobs as it is. No, I don't mind paying. What I object to is that they're trying to charge me for something I didn't order—something that wasn't used in the play at all, and what's more, the most expensive thing of the whole bill. It isn't very much, but I object to the thing on principle."

"Which is the firm in question?"

"Bradworthy's—I expect you know the name. Their address is somewhere near Drury Lane. If it interests you, I'll look for the bill, and show you what it's all about."

"You needn't trouble yourself," said Mallett. "I can tell you. Bradworthy's are dunning you for a brown beard and a padded suit, supplied by them to the London and Imperial Estates Ltd., some time between August and October last."

Lord Bernard looked at him in amazement.

"You are perfectly right," he said. "But how on earth you could guess is utterly beyond me. No, don't tell me. I prefer to remain in ignorant admiration, 'to venerate where I cannot presently comprehend', as Burke so prettily said of the British constitution. I shall dine out on this story for weeks."

He shook the inspector's hand warmly.

"Good-bye," he said, "and thank you for a most amusing morning. I wish you could tell me just one thing, though."

"What is that?"

"Ought I to pay Bradworthy's bill or not? It is rather on my conscience."

"I must leave that to your lordship's solicitors," said Mallett, and took his departure.

21

At Mrs. Bradworthy's

Old Mrs. Bradworthy was an institution in theatrical London. She had sat, a genial fat figure in black silk, at the back of her little shop, just round the corner from Drury Lane, longer than the most elderly *ingénue* actress could remember. It was a gloomy shop, the light from the windows being all but cut off by the suits of stage armour which hung facing the street, and had so hung, growing daily dirtier, ever since they were made for Irving's production of *Macbeth*. Mallett had been there once or twice before—although the interest of the detective in make-up and disguise is not nearly so great as is often supposed—and he never ceased to marvel that so small a place could hold the vast stock of dresses, wigs and stage accessories without which no amateur play-producing society, no pageant or fancy-dress ball could hope to be successful. It was a wonder, too, that even the proprietress, inured as she was to the blackness in which she lived, could find her way about. The unwary visitor, straying in the dingy recesses at the back of the shop, could be fortunate if he did not break his knees over some "property" or another on the floor, or bump his head on a pantomime mask hanging unseen from above; but Mrs. Bradworthy, guided by some instinct of her own, would go at once to the mustiest corner in her establishment and bring from it at the first attempt exactly what the most exotic fancy of her customer required. She had lived so long in the atmosphere of the stage that she and everything about her seemed a trifle unreal. The very assistants in the shop looked more like supers than ordinary human beings. Only her charges were firmly related to the workaday world, and these, Mallett knew, were no joke. One does not become an institution in trade—even when that trade is a theatrical one—without a keen sense of business.

He found the old lady sitting behind the counter, working, as usual, on her endless accounts. She greeted him with pleasure.

"Well, Mr. Mallett, this is a nice surprise! What can I do for you today?"

"I've called about Lord Bernard Gaveston's account," began the inspector.

"Lord Bernard, indeed!" The old lady took him up at once. "Why can't he pay, I want to know? It isn't becoming a gentleman, let alone a lord, to keep me out of my money all this time."

"I wonder if you'd let me look at his account," said Mallett, diplomatically avoiding taking sides in the controversy. "There's one item in it that interests me a little."

With surprising strength for her age the old lady instantly reached down a heavy ledger from a shelf behind her, and quickly found the place.

"Here you are," she said, pushing it over to the inspector. "Can you read it all right there, or do you want the electric light? I'll turn it on if you like, but—"

"No, no, I can see perfectly," Mallett lied. Mrs. Bradworthy's parsimony was notorious, and he knew that she would never forgive him if he proved himself to be wasteful in the matter of electric current. Straining his eyes over the page, he found the item he sought.

"That is what I am enquiring about," he said. "The padded suit and beard."

Mrs. Bradworthy shook her head sadly, and clicked her tongue against her teeth.

"Tck, tck! The most expensive thing in the whole account! Bought, and not hired like the rest of them, you see, Mr. Mallett. It's a bad business—it should never have gone out without payment, but there it is. It will be a lesson to us, that's all I can say."

"I notice that it is dated a few days later than the other items," Mallett remarked.

"Yes, indeed. It was ordered special, after the others had gone out. I remember it particularly. In a great hurry, it was. And then to try and get out of paying for it! It really seems criminal, doesn't it?"

"Did you take the order yourself?"

"Indeed, yes. Over the telephone—nasty new-fangled thing, and such an expense too, you wouldn't believe."

"But who actually gave the order?"

"Why, Lord Bernard—or I suppose it was. I didn't take much notice, naturally. But he said Lord Bernard's account, as clear as I'm talking to you."

"And it was delivered—to whom?"

"It wasn't delivered at all. It was fetched, that very evening."

Mallett could hardly restrain his impatience.

"Who fetched it?" he asked.

Mrs. Bradworthy shook her head.

"It was late, I know," she said. "After I'd gone home, because I remember getting it out and doing up the parcel myself, before I left. You can't trust these girls to do anything properly if you don't do it yourself. But as for who actually handed it over, so to speak, now you're asking. Amelia!"

A tall, ungainly, myoptic woman of uncertain age emerged from the dim background of the shop in answer to her call.

"Amelia, dear, that padded suit of Lord Bernard's—were you there when it was fetched?"

"No, Mrs. Bradworthy. It was very late, after I'd gone. I know that, because Tom complained to me next day he'd been kept from shutting up by waiting for the gentleman. Five minutes after closing time he came in, Tom told me."

"Then it was Tom who handed the parcel over?" said Mallett.

"Yes, that's right," said Mrs. Bradworthy in a peculiar tone of mournful satisfaction. "It must have been old Tom."

"It was Tom all right," echoed Amelia.

"Then Tom can tell us who actually took the parcel away," Mallett exclaimed. He had no sooner uttered the words than he felt as if he had committed a blasphemy. Mrs. Bradworthy's face took on an expression of pained reproach and Amelia looked as though she were about to cry.

"Oh, but haven't you heard, Mr. Mallett?" Mrs. Bradworthy asked softly. "Poor old Tom—twenty-five years he'd been here—and then, only last week—those dreadful motor cars!"

Mallett's hopes evaporated into thin air.

"So Tom is dead?" he said dully.

Mrs. Bradworthy nodded. Amelia blew her nose loudly and faded away.

"I see. Good afternoon, Mrs. Bradworthy, and thank you."

"But what I want to know is, will Lord Bernard pay my bill or not?" asked Mrs. Bradworthy, overcoming her emotion with remarkable speed.

For the second time that day Mallett ended an interview on an unanswered question. He made his way back to Scotland Yard, oppressed with the strong realization that the evidence on which he had so confidently depended had failed him, and that all was to do again.

22

Arrest

Sergeant Frant was busy, and perfectly happy. He kept the telephone fully employed on long-distance calls and was perpetually in and out of Mallett's room, each time with a fresh piece of news to report. The inspector paid little attention. For the whole morning he sat at his desk, hunched up over a pile of documents, going over the statements of witnesses, the depositions at the inquest and his own memoranda. He refused the assistance which Frant offered him.

"There's a link missing," was all he would say, "and it's somewhere here. I must find it myself."

After a solitary lunch, he came back looking better pleased with himself. Frant met him on the stairs.

"I'm just going—" he began with a triumphant air.

"Can you tell me," Mallett interrupted unceremoniously, "where Crabtree is to be found now?"

"Yes. He's got a job in a wholesale fruiterer's at Covent Garden."

"Thanks. Where did you say you were going?"

"To Bow Street."

214

"Then I'll come with you."

At the bottom of Bow Street, Frant indicated where the fruiterer in question was to be found, and the men parted. Mallett discovered Crabtree, a pile of orange-boxes on his head, on the pavement outside the shop. The man gave him a sour look as he recognized him.

"What is it this time?" he snarled.

"Just a question," said Mallett genially. "You needn't stop your work to answer it."

"Then get out o' the way!" Crabtree began to walk beneath his precarious load to a van drawn up some distance away. Mallett fell into step with him, as though interviewing in these circumstances was the most ordinary thing in the world.

"When you were with Mr. James," he asked, "do you ever remember seeing him with an umbrella?"

"No!" The orange-boxes crashed down into the van by way of emphasis.

"Ah, I thought not. I just wanted to make sure. Good day!"

Crabtree scratched his head, now relieved of its burden, and informed the world in general that he, Crabtree, was several unprintable things; by which he was quite correctly understood by his friends to mean that he was rather more than mildly surprised.

Mallett meanwhile was making the best of his way towards Bramston's Inn, the address of the only one of Ballantine's concerns outside the offices of the "Twelve Apostles" in Lothbury. It is not very far from Covent Garden as the crow flies. As the Londoner walks, it is apt to be a tedious and tiresome journey, punctuated by the exploration of blind alleys and vain appeals for directions addressed to passers-by, who invariably prove to be themselves "strangers in these parts." Mallett, who enjoyed nothing so much as threading with secure knowledge the by-ways of London—his "Forty-two routes from the Old Bailey to Scotland Yard" was a minor classic in police literature—covered the distance speedily enough. His way led across Kingsway, through the pleasant spaces of Lincoln's Inn Fields, through Old Square and out into Chancery Lane under the archway on which Ben Jonson is said to have toiled as a bricklayer. Then he plunged into the network of narrow streets that lies between Fleet Street and Holborn. It is a region dominated by great printing works, its tortuous ways clogged by newspaper vans and horse-drawn drays, hiding in odd corners shy little chop-houses beloved of journalists, a house or two where history has been made and not merely recorded, and what must surely be the last row of cottage-gardens in Central London. Somewhere East of Fetter Lane the inspector turned sharply down an alley to his right, ducked under the nose of a cart-horse in a warehouse entry, directed two lost Americans to Gough Square, turned to his left through a passage that seemed no more than a slit in the wall, veered right once more and finally came to a standstill facing the short row of early Georgian houses that bears the name of Bramston's Inn.

Topographers and historians are unable to say for certain whether or not the Inn has any valid connection with that Sir John Bramston who was Chief Justice to Charles I. It was, say some, in its earlier days, an Inn of Chancery—a poor relation of the opulent and flourishing Inns of Court, and indeed it still wears a faint family resemblance to its more famous cousins. But it is a resemblance that has grown more and more distant with time. Hall and chapel have long since been swept away and now the only legal flavour that yet remains to its dark chambers and ruinous staircases is supplied by two firms of solicitors, neither of them of very high repute. For the rest, its tenants are obscurely charitable societies, minor trade associations and firms of uncertain reputation—such as, for example, the Anglo-Dutch Rubber and General Trading Syndicate.

The name, in dirty black paint upon a dirty yellow background, was still legible in the doorway of one of the four houses that made up the row. The offices were on the fourth floor, and from the dusty windows hung a board which announced: "These desirable offices to let. Apply caretaker." The caretaker, a shabby, ill-shaven man with red and suspicious eyes, emerged from the basement at Mallett's knock.

"Police?" he said querulously, in reply to the inspector's summons. "We've 'ad 'em 'ere already. They didn't find nothing."

"All the same, I'll have a look round, if you don't mind," answered Mallett.

They ascended the stairs together and went into the deserted office. It consisted of two rooms only, unfurnished save for a couple of desks and a safe, the door of which swung open to reveal the emptiness within. Mallett walked quickly round them, his footsteps sounding heavily on the uncarpeted floor, while the caretaker watched him from the door. In the furthest angle of the inner room was a window, giving on to the back of the block. Mallett threw it open.

"What's this?" he demanded.

"Fire escape. They put it in—the Anglo-Dutch people did—soon after they took it."

The inspector leant out of the window and gazed thoughtfully down the narrow iron staircase. From the angle at which the window was set, it could not be overlooked in any way by neighbouring tenants. The wall of No. 3, next door, shrugged a protective shoulder which effectually screened it from observation. The wall of the building opposite was blank. He considered. That should be Black Dog Court below, and from it, he knew, a passage ran into Fleet Street. It was a well-devised back exit—or entry. He nodded in satisfaction and withdrew.

" 'Ave you seen all you want to see?" asked the man behind him.

"I've seen all there is to see here," returned Mallett, "but there's still one thing not here I want to see. Will you show it to me?"

"What's that?"

"The umbrella."

"What are you talking about? What umbrella?"

"The umbrella which was left behind here the last time the tenant left this place."

The man became talkative all at once.

"I don't know nothing about no umbrella!" he cried. "Straight I don't! I don't know what you're getting at, guv'nor! I've bin 'ere, a man and boy, thirty years, and I've never so much as seen no umbrella! You ask any of the tenants 'ereabouts, they'll tell you the sort of man I am—"

Meanwhile, Mallett, holding his arm in a firm but gentle grip, was impelling him slowly downstairs.

"An umbrella," he murmured in his blandest tones, while the caretaker's protests died away into whimperings. "A nice silk umbrella. With a broad gold band on it, for certain. And initials. Or perhaps a name and address on it. Oh, certainly, a name and address I should think. Where is it?"

They had reached the bottom landing. With a convulsive start, the man tore himself away from the inspector's grasp and vanished into his dim abode below stairs. There was the sound of chairs being overset by hasty movements, of a key being turned in a lock, of a cupboard door opening and closing with a bang, and the man returned. He was pale with fear, and in a hand that trembled violently he extended to the detective an umbrella, precisely as had been described.

"Thank you," said Mallett coolly. "That was what I had in mind." He inspected the gold band that decorated the handle. "Name and address in full, I see. Just as I thought. Well, well!"

"I didn't mean to keep it, guv'nor," the caretaker insisted.

"No?"

"No. Yer see, it was like this. After Anglo-Dutch hadn't been near the place two, three days or more, I thought I'd just go up to see if things was all right, see? And I found that there umbrella put away, like, be'ind the door. I didn't look at the name on the 'andle or anythink, I just thought I'd keep it by me for 'im when 'e come back. Then the police coming in and all, I took another look at it, and when I seed 'oo it belonged to I got scared. I didn't know what to do about it. I didn't dare let on I'd got it, even."

His eyes anxiously sought Mallett's to see if he was believed. "I—I swear I never done nothink wrong, guv'nor," he went on. "Only just what I told you, that's all."

Mallett cut him short with a "That'll do!" The story might be true or not. He had sufficient experience of the terror that certain classes feel towards anything connected with the police to be prepared to credit it. But it was of little moment whether the man was lying or speaking the truth, now that he had provided the essential evidence.

"You talk about 'Anglo-Dutch' as if he was a person," he said. "Did only one man use these offices, then?"

"At the start there was two or three used to come in and out, when they was moving in. After that there was only just the one. I never found out 'is name—that's why I called 'im Anglo-Dutch."

"Did he come regularly?"

"Most days—not every day. 'E'd come in the morning, ten o'clock or thereabouts, and leave in the evening. I never seed 'im go out to lunch, even. I used to wonder what 'e did there all day by 'isself. 'E never 'ad no callers."

Mallett produced a photograph from his pocket.

"Did he look anything like this?" he asked.

The caretaker peered at it doubtfully.

"I'm a bit short-sighted," he confessed. "I wouldn't like to swear that's the same man, not on oath, I wouldn't."

"But is it like him?"

"Oh, yes, it's like 'im all right. The same sort of man, you might say. But it's no good asking me to swear—"

"I'm not," said Mallett curtly, and strode away.

But for all the sharpness of his words, his heart was singing. For the photograph he had shown to the caretaker was a copy of the police photograph of Mr. Colin James, and the umbrella under his arm was the umbrella of Lionel Ballantine.

Frank Harper was walking aimlessly up Fleet Street. His expression, as he turned into a tobacconist's shop, was decidedly more clouded than that of a happily engaged young man should ordinarily be. He told himself, as he bought his cigarettes, that he was smoking a great deal too much. It was not the first time within the last few days that he had made the same reflection, and it had always ended in his going out somewhere and buying another packet. For whatever the voice of common sense might say, in the long run it was always his overstrained nerves that had the last word and drove him to seek relief. Even then, he knew, no relief could be anything but temporary, so long as the essential cause of the trouble remained unresolved. It lay in his pocket now, that cause, as it had lain for two days past—a letter from the girl he loved, asking, and asking insistently, the one question which he could not answer. And this morning another had been added to it, reproaching him for his failure to reply. Another would come soon, he knew—perhaps it would be a little more bitter than the last. And he, who had so lately been lifted to the summit of happiness, now saw himself travelling down a long slope leading to an inevitable quarrel—an estrangement, even. "If you won't tell me, I can't marry you!" Would it come to that? He shrugged his shoulders as he lit his cigarette. Well, if it came to that, it came to that! Meanwhile, there was nothing to do about it—except to smoke incessantly, and hope fervently that it wouldn't. If a girl can't trust a man, he thought bitterly—but what if a man can't trust himself?

As he walked out of the shop he jostled a burly figure on the pavement. He murmured a perfunctory "Sorry!" and walked on. The man he had touched turned at the sound of his voice and walked quickly after him.

"Mr. Harper, isn't it?" he said.

Harper looked round. For a moment or two he gazed blankly at the large man with the smart umbrella who had accosted him. Then a look of recognition came into his face.

"Ah, yes, of course. Inspector Mallett," he murmured in his somewhat irritatingly superior manner.

Mallett's eyes gazed keenly into the young man's. For a fraction of a second there was a trace of disappointment in his expression, as though he failed to find what he had sought there. Then a smile illuminated his broad features.

"This is a bit of luck," he exclaimed genially. "You're just the fellow I wanted to see."

"You know my address, I think, if you wish to ask me anything," returned the other coolly.

"No time like the present, though, is there?" said Mallett, unrebuffed. "I tell you what—I'm due at the Yard. If you're not doing anything, why not share a taxi down there? We can have a little chat as we go."

The smart umbrella was waved in the air, and a cab drew up at the pavement. Mallett flung open the door for Harper to get in. Harper hesitated a moment, looked up into the inspector's still smiling face, then nodded abruptly and climbed into the vehicle. The door closed and the taxi moved off. A young reporter on an evening paper happened to see them go.

"Did you see that?" he said to a friend. "Inspector Mallett! He's made an arrest!"

But it was Sergeant Frant, not Inspector Mallett, who was to make an arrest that day. His incessant labours had borne fruit. They had, to begin with, brought about a considerable liveliness in a quiet part of Yorkshire, involving not only the police, but also doctors, clergymen, registrars and asylum officials. The enquiries that Mr. Elderson had made quietly and unofficially were repeated with thoroughness and such dispatch that about the time that Mallett was entering Bramston's Inn, Frant, in a police car, was turning into Mount Street, bearing in his pocket a fateful slip of paper, signed by the chief magistrate at Bow Street. He was just in time to see Captain Eales, a small suitcase in his hand, emerge from a house door, and step into a taxi which was waiting for him. The cab gathered speed slowly, and with the police car in its wake, drove off. As Frant had anticipated, it took a northerly direction, and in due time it drew up outside a pleasant little detached house in St. John's Wood. Frant gave a quiet order to his driver, and the car slowed down close to the kerb, just giving him time to alight so that he touched the pavement almost at the same moment as did his quarry, fifty yards ahead. Then it drove on, past the house, turned into a side street, reversed and awaited further orders, just out of sight.

Frant strolled towards Eales, his pulses quickening slightly with the uncontrollable excitement of the hunter. But the latter instead of paying the cab, as he had expected, walked straight up to the front door of the house, leaving his suitcase behind him in the waiting vehicle. The sergeant judged it wise to hold his hand. He allowed Eales to enter the house unmolested, walked on past him to the corner, turned and came slowly back. He had not proceeded far when Eales emerged once more from the house. On the steps he turned, and called out to someone behind him: "Mind you, this is the last time!" Frant caught a glimpse of Du Pine standing in the porch, could just distinguish the expressionless smile which greeted the words, and then the door closed.

By the time Eales had given his order to the driver and had settled himself again on the seat of the taxi, the police car had been summoned and the sedate pursuit began anew. This time the course lay southward. The little procession of two skirted Lord's cricket ground, ran down Regent's Park Road, crossed the Marylebone Road and went on down Baker Street and across Oxford Street towards the West End. The chase ended just off Piccadilly, at the headquarters of an air line to the Continent. There Frant tapped his man on the shoulder as he was about to climb into a motor-coach bound for Croydon aerodrome, and murmured a few words in his ear which caused him to abandon the idea of flying for that day.

Eales, a little pale but perfectly self-possessed, entered the police car with a shrug of his thin shoulders.

"You have got the warrant, I suppose?" he asked Frant as they started for Bow Street.

Frant read it over to him. The effect was somewhat strange.

"Bigamy!" exclaimed the prisoner. "Oh, my God!" He laughed aloud above the noise of the traffic.

The rest of the journey was accomplished in silence, but in the charge-room at Bow Street Eales spoke once more.

"I suppose that damned little double-crosser Du Pine is responsible for this?" he demanded.

"I am not allowed to tell you through what channels information reaches the police," answered Frant warily.

"Because if he is, I can tell you a thing or two—"

The sergeant cut him short and at once administered the statutory caution. Eales, a little impressed by the official verbiage, fell silent once more. Frant watched him narrowly.

"I think I am entitled to tell you," he said in detached tones, "that we are a little interested in a trip abroad you made on the night of the 13th of November. But of course if you prefer to say nothing, you are perfectly entitled—"

The prisoner's face changed.

"Here, give me a pen and paper!" he snarled.

He began to write, copiously, fluently, pausing only at intervals to swear under his breath.

23

Success

The taxi wound its way slowly through the thronging traffic. The gloom of a late winter afternoon had set in, and the street lamps, which had just been lighted, only illuminated fitfully the corner in which Harper sat. Mallett looked at him curiously. The pose suggested to his experienced eyes a sense of strain, as though the young man was compelling himself to appear at ease, without altogether succeeding. His head lolled back comfortably enough against the back of the car, his legs were jauntily crossed, but at the same time there was to a close observer a rigidity in the body which told of muscles that were taut with the effort of doing nothing, of nerves protesting against the ordeal to which they were being subjected. None the less, the inspector looked in vain for any sign of the acute terror which their encounter at Brighton had so unmistakably inspired. Then he had been frightened—horror-struck, almost; now he was ill at ease, nervous perhaps, but no more. Here was an enigma, and one that the inspector determined to resolve without delay.

"The last time I saw you," he began, "you seemed to be enjoying yourself."

"Enjoying myself?" echoed Harper in apparent surprise. "That seems rather an odd way of putting it."

"I don't see anything odd about it," returned Mallett. "It would have been my idea of enjoying myself, at your age, and most people's too."

"People's ideas of enjoyment evidently differ. I really can't answer for yours. Personally, I found it a most distasteful experience, and I thought I made it clear at the time."

"No, I'm damned if you did!" exclaimed Mallett, irritated at this absurd piece of fencing. "If ever I saw a young couple enjoying themselves—"

"Really, Inspector," Harper broke in, "I think we are talking at cross-purposes. Now I come to think of it, you mentioned the last time you saw me. Strictly speaking, I have no idea when that was. As a detective you may, for all I know, make a practice of seeing people when they aren't looking. I can only speak of the last time I saw you, and that was at the inquest."

The taxi travelled some distance before Mallett found words to answer this extraordinary assertion.

"Are you going to deny that you were at the Riviera Hotel, Brighton, the evening after the inquest?" he asked sternly.

"Certainly not. Why should I?"

"And that you saw me there—in the interval between two dances—and seeing me, showed every sign of surprise and fright, and"—he paused for greater emphasis—"and guilt?"

Harper's manner had changed completely. Abandoning altogether his attitude of defensive suspicion, he now leant forward and spoke with an appearance of entire sincerity.

"Look here, sir," he said. "I don't in the least understand what you are driving at. I was at the hotel on
that evening. I was dancing. I was enjoying myself very
much. As for being frightened or guilty, I never felt less
like it in my life. You tell me that you saw me. Well,
you can take my word for it that I did not see you. Now,
will you please tell me what all this means?"

"You did see me," Mallett maintained. "I was standing
within a few yards of you—just behind you, in fact."

"Which of course explains why I didn't see you."

"You were looking in a glass to tie your bow-tie. It
was at that moment that you saw me and looked—as I
have said—frightened and guilty."

"Looking in the glass to tie my tie . . ." The young
man mused a moment. "Good lord, so that was it?"

"Ah, so you remember now?"

"Certainly I remember—not seeing you, though. I
may have, of course, but your face made absolutely no
impression on me."

"Then what was there to be frightened of?"

"I was frightened", said Harper soberly, "of myself."

"What?"

"Of my own appearance, I mean. That bow-tie. Don't
you remember, Inspector, the day we found him there—
at Daylesford Gardens—I commented to you about his
tie—what an ugly thing it was, and how badly tied?
Well, when I looked in the glass, I got the shock of my
life. Mine looked exactly like it. It suddenly brought it
all back to me—that horrible swollen face and how his
tongue stuck out from the corner of his mouth—ugh!"

Mallett was laughing.

"So that was why you looked so scared!" he chuckled.
"Well, well! I always said you knew something about this
case we didn't know! What a lot of trouble you might
have spared us!"

"Trouble? You don't really mean that tie business was important?"

"About the most important thing in the whole case."

"I don't understand. Please tell me."

Mallett had no objection. It was a minor point—now. He was relieved to find that this likeable young fellow was free from suspicion, and success had loosened his tongue.

"Your tie looked odd", he explained, "because someone else had just tried to tie it for you—and done it very badly."

"Yes," said Harper, blushing a little in spite of himself.

"Ballantine's looked odd for just the same reason."

"But why should anyone tie it for him?"

"For the same reason that he put on his coat and trousers for him—to make him look like Ballantine."

"After he was dead, do you mean?"

"Precisely."

"Then what," Harper asked with growing excitement, "what did he look like before he was killed?"

"He looked remarkably like a stout gentleman with a beard who once came to your office to take a furnished house in South Kensington."

"Do you mean, then," the young man breathed in a voice hardly above a whisper, "that James was Ballantine?"

"I do. A fact," added Mallett, "which is going to prove very inconvenient to a number of otherwise excellent alibis."

There was silence between them as the car crossed the end of Trafalgar Square and sped along Whithall.

"Of course," murmured Harper, "I always thought that couldn't have been his tie. Nobody could have worn one that colour with those clothes. I wonder why he changed it." He shivered and then seemed to rouse himself suddenly from his reflections. "I'll get out here, if you don't mind," he said. "That is, unless you want—"

"That's all right," said the inspector. "You've told me all I wanted to know, and very interesting it was."

He ordered the driver to stop, put Harper down, and drove on alone into New Scotland Yard. He was feeling in a genial mood, expansive and self-satisfied. The chase was almost at an end and he was about to reap the reward of his persistence and ingenuity. It did not occur to him to look back at his late companion. Had he done so, he would have seen him stand a moment irresolute on the pavement, and then go quickly to a public telephone box.

Mallett made his way at once to his office. As he entered it, he was overtaken by Frant, in a high state of excitement. He motioned him to come in.

"Well?" he asked.

"I arrested Eales this afternoon," said the sergeant.

"Yes? Is that all?"

"And Du Pine half an hour later."

The inspector smiled. "More bigamy?" he asked.

Frant shook his head. "You may laugh, sir," he said, "but that charge of bigamy has worked like a charm."

"I'm sure it has. But what exactly is Du Pine's offence?"

"Drug-trafficking."

"Aha! So that was his little game, was it?"

"Yes. He'd been importing it on quite a large scale for some time apparently, and latterly employing Eales as his messenger to Paris. The poor devil was so hard up he couldn't refuse, he tells me, and he was quite well paid. When I arrested him this morning he was just off on another trip—by air this time."

"The infernal cheek of that fellow Du Pine—right under our noses!"

"It was rather more than just cheek," said the sergeant gently. "You see, he had to get the stuff—he wanted it, desperately."

"For his own use, you mean?"

Frant nodded. "He was in a ghastly state when he was brought in," he went on. "The station doctor had to give him a pretty stiff dose of morphia or he'd have gone off his head. I really felt sorry for the blackguard. It seems that he's been an addict for years, but since the crash of the company and Ballantine's death, worry and fright have so wrecked his nerves that he's been increasing the doses until he'd used up all his supply—and his customers' too. That's why he sent Eales over today. It's a very useful capture, and if the French police play up, we ought to be able to round up a whole gang on both sides of the Channel."

Mallett rubbed his hands in satisfaction.

"The end of a perfect day," he purred. "I think we've both earned a cup of tea."

"And now," said Frant as they sat down to tea, "would you mind telling me, just for my own information, what you have done and just how you managed to get to the bottom of this?"

"Pure—what is the word?—ratiocination," answered the inspector proudly. "I approached it this way. There were several people who might have killed Ballantine. Of them all the one who took my fancy from the start was Fanshawe. Apart from the question of motive, he was the only man who seemed to me to be of the stuff of which murderers are made. Not that he is a common sort of killer by any means; on the contrary, I should put him down as a distinctly superior type—high-minded, fastidious, and all the rest of it. But vain, Frant, vain—or, if that's too small a word, proud as Lucifer. The sort of man who, if he decided that someone else ought to

230

be wiped out would think no more of doing it than of squashing a fly on the window-pane. That was my first reflection.

"Then I went on to consider the evidence. One thing struck me at once. Fanshawe went to France by the night boat on Friday the 13th. So, we found, did Eales. A coincidence, no doubt, but a perfectly possible one. But so also did Colin James. That struck me as a perfectly impossible coincidence—that three individuals, connected with this crime, should all have chosen independently to travel by that boat. Now we know, had known from the start, that James was someone else in disguise. It stuck out a mile. To reduce my three travellers to two, my impossible coincidence to a possible one, James must be one of the others in disguise, either Eales or Fanshawe. I struck out Eales, for reasons which you know. Therefore James was Fanshawe. At the same time, we knew on irrefutable evidence that James had been a tenant in Daylesford Gardens while Fanshawe was a tenant of a cell in Maidstone. Therefore James was not Fanshawe. Two perfectly logical propositions arriving at opposite results. I left them there and went back to consider what we have always regarded as the crux of the problem, the identity of James.

"Who had I got to look for? Either somebody who had disappeared altogether, about the time that James came to life, or somebody whose manner of living enabled him to lead a double life, putting in sufficient appearances in his old haunts and under his normal guise to avoid suspicion, while spending the rest of his time building up the new identity of Colin James. I went through the records of disappearances, and found none that would suit. I was not surprised. James had been only intermittently at Daylesford Gardens, and I suspected all along that he had been spending the rest of his time elsewhere in another identity. So I had to find someone whose conduct had recently been irregular and abnormal, whose sleeping places one couldn't trace, and who had a motive for building up another personality at the time in question. I found him—Lionel Ballantine.

"Once that was established, the rest fell into place easily enough. The letter to the bank, the uneasiness of Mrs. Eales, everything was explained. Then I turned back to the first part of the problem, and that fell into place too. James was Fanshawe; James was Ballantine. Why not, when it was simply a case of taking a disguise off a dead man and putting it on a live one? It only remained to prove it, and that turned out to be the difficulty. Unexpectedly, I wasn't able to prove what I know to be the fact, that Ballantine ordered James's suit from Mrs. Bradworthy, but my second shot turned out a winner. The evidence at the inquest was that Ballantine left his office with his umbrella. No umbrella was found with him at Daylesford Gardens. Therefore he must have left it behind when he changed into James. I pondered over various possible places which he could have used for the job, and hit on the Anglo-Dutch offices, which seemed to have no other purpose in life. As it turned out I was right."

He brandished the umbrella in triumph.

"A pretty little thing, isn't it?" he remarked. "Strictly, I suppose, it belongs to the creditors, but I should love to keep it. It would be a pity to make a hole in such a nice piece of silk, though. But just as a memento, I think I must have it."

"I've got my own memento," said Frant. "I shall frame this."

He held up a scribbled sheet of paper.

"Identity of Colin James.

"The following are the names of the chief suspects in the case of Lionel Ballantine: X

Eales
Du Pine
Fanshawe
Harper
Crabtree

"James was a mask for Ballantine. The mask survived the wearer!—J.M."

Mallett laughed.

"That was a piece of conceit on my part," he said. "But I was so pleased when I had seen through the problem that I couldn't resist the temptation of mystifying you. Well, the case is at an end now, I suppose, so far as detection is concerned. Tomorrow I shall apply for another warrant at Bow Street and after that the lawyers take charge. Do you know, Frant, in some ways I feel quite sorry—"

There was a knock at the door.

"Come in!"

24

Escape

Mallett was not a superstitious man, but he always declared that from the moment he heard that knock at the door he felt confident that something had gone wrong. Certainly there was no excuse for the glare which he fixed on the man who now came into the room—a perfectly common-place plain-clothes detective.

"What do you want?" he barked.

"I was told to report to you sir," was the reply.

"Told to report—who by?"

"By the Deputy Commissioner, sir."

Mallett looked at him more closely.

"I don't understand. Weren't you on duty at Daylesford Court Mansions?"

"I was, sir."

"Well? Who has relieved you?"

"Nobody, sir. I was simply ordered to cease keeping observation and report to you."

"What?" cried Mallett, leaping from his chair.

"I understand there was a special instruction to that effect from the Home Secretary," the man continued.

" 'I always treated him very decently when he was my fag at school,' " murmured Frant with a wry smile, but the inspector did not heed him. With a roar he dashed from the room and sped along the corridor, leaving Frant and the bewildered newcomer to follow as best they could.

They came up with him in the entrance. He had stopped there abruptly, his great shoulders heaving as he recovered his breath. When the sergeant approached, he caught his arm and held it tightly.

"I'm a fool, Frant," he muttered. "My nerve must be going. We said to-morrow, didn't we? There's no real hurry, now, just because of this piece of imbecility. It's only—only damnably upsetting."

"Quite, quite," said Frant soothingly.

"When you've got a rat in a trap, it's a bit of a jar to find that some fool has opened the trap while your back's turned," he went on, "even though the rat doesn't know it is in a trap. I'm not going to risk it, Frant. We're going to Daylesford Court Mansions now."

Within a few moments a police car swung out into Whitehall, carrying the three officers. They were silent as they drove. It had begun to rain, and the pavements were bright with the reflections of the street-lamps. On such a night, Mallett reflected, Ballantine had walked with another to his death in the little house in the quiet Kensington square. They passed the entrance to Daylesford Gardens, and, craning his neck, he could just distinguish the house itself, now dark and tenantless. It was only a matter of a few hundred yards, and they were at the Mansions. Strange, that the tale should end so near to where it had begun.

Daylesford Court Mansions have little in common with the "luxury flats" of modern London. They boast neither lifts nor uniformed porters, and there were no curious eyes to watch the detectives as they entered. Mallett clattered up the stone stairs at their head. The inhospitable entrance, the hygienically glazed walls put him in mind of a prison. Did Fanshawe, he wondered as he went, ever note the resemblance? Prison! Well, he would resume his acquaintance with that before long—for a little time, and then—he felt a little nauseated. Not for the first time, on such an occasion, he was conscious of a sense of disgust with himself for the duty he was about to perform. To deliver a man over to the hangman in order to expiate a wholly worthless life—it seemed an ignoble task, when all was said. In a perfectly organized community, a man like Ballantine would have been removed long ago, while Fanshawe—

His fingers closed over the door-knocker of Miss Fanshawe's flat. The touch of the cold metal served to dispel at once all introspection. While there was something to be done, he could leave it to others to decide the purpose or utility of the deed. "Now for it," he said to himself, and knocked long and loud.

The summons was answered after a short delay by a tall, grim, middle-aged woman, pale of countenance, her lips set in a firm line. She wore an apron which seemed incongruous alike to her well-made dress and her authoritative manner.

She greeted the detectives with raised eyebrows and a slightly contemptuous "Yes?"

"I am a police officer—" Mallett began.

"Very well. You wish to see my brother, I suppose."

"Is he here?"

"Certainly." Her lip curled as though at the suggestion that he should have run away. "He has been in his room for the last hour. I will show you the way. The maid is out at the present," she added. The last piece of information was evidently intended to explain why she should be doing them this service in person.

The three men entered the flat and Miss Fanshawe strode stiffly in front of them down the narrow passage. Presently she stopped at a door, knocked smartly at it, opened it wide, called out: "Some policemen to see you, John!" and walked on without herself crossing the threshold.

Mallett was the first to enter the room, with Frant close at his heels. It was a plainly furnished bedroom, with an open desk in one corner. On the desk lay a large white envelope. On the bed lay John Fanshawe. An empty glass was beside him. He was fully dressed, except for his shoes, which he had considerately taken off and left on the floor. He had died painlessly, and if his unfurrowed brow was any guide, with an easy conscience.

Frant broke the news to Miss Fanshawe. He found her in the kitchen, preparing supper. She heard him without the slightest trace of emotion.

"He always said he would do this, rather than go to prison again," was her only comment. "He didn't tell me you were coming for him, but I'm not surprised."

"Is there anything I—we can do for you?" stammered the sergeant, taken aback.

"Nothing, thank you." Then with a muttered "One must eat," she turned to her cooking again.

The inspector, having made arrangements for the removal of the body, turned his attention to the papers in the desk. He observed that the letter was addressed to himself, and characteristically left it to the last. Quickly he sorted out the neatly filed documents, appraised their significance, and divided them into two little heaps— those of value from the police point of view and those that could be disregarded. Among the former were two bank passbooks which he scrutinized with some care and not a little surprise. Finally, when he was satisfied that nothing of interest had been overlooked, he opened the letter.

"Well, Inspector," it began abruptly, "so you have solved the problem! My congratulations! In an hour or so, perhaps less, I suppose you will be clumping up here in your heavy policeman's boots, all agog to make your arrest and provide a bit more carrion for the gallows. But when you come, I shall not be here. It would have been easy enough for me to absent myself in body as well as—if a policeman can understand the word—in soul, but I shall not attempt to. At my time of life I am not going to embark on a wretched game of hide-and-seek abroad, skulking in third-rate hotels under an assumed name, with the long drawn out mummery of extradition at the end of it all. I loathe an anticlimax, and two little tablets which I bought in Paris will save me from that. Candidly, I should like to have gone on living, merely for the intellectual pleasure of having got the better of you. Since that is denied, there is no great point in further existence. And to the last I retain the far greater pleasure of leaving the world a better place for the extermination of a rogue.

"How did you find it out, I wonder? I am honestly surprised that you did, for it seems to me to have been as nearly perfect a crime as is possible in an imperfect world. I take no credit for it, for the planning, after all, was all his. I merely took advantage of a heaven-sent chance. It must be uncommon for a man to provide an alibi for his own executioner. The whole affair was quite simple, really. As I told you, I saw Ballantine for a moment at his office on Friday morning, 13th November. As I did not tell you, I saw him again that evening. I was going home, and at the corner of Upper Daylesford Street I almost ran into him. He knew me, of course, and the

238

start he gave was enough for me to know him. I think I should have recognized him in any case. When you have been seeing the same face in your dreams for four years, it takes more than a sham beard and a big paunch to deceive you. I challenged him—told him I should give him away unless he gave me what I wanted, and to my surprise he took me with him to the house in Daylesford Gardens. As soon as we got inside, he asked me how much I wanted. I named a modest figure and he sat down at his desk to write a cheque. The poor fool! As if money could have satisfied me! He soon found out his mistake. He sat with his back to me to write and it was a simple matter to pull the cord off the blind and slip it round his neck. It was the best moment of my life.

"It was only when I began to go through his things that I realized my amazing good fortune. He had planned to leave the country that very night, and had made all his arrangements accordingly. In his bag I found a couple of hundred pounds in notes and enough in bearer bonds for all my purposes. There was Colin James's passport, there were James's tickets, James's reserved places on the train and boat, a note of James's hotel in Paris, and—on the body—James's clothes and beard. It was all too easy. All I had to do was to turn James back into Ballantine. That was simple enough, except that the dressy beast had worn a stock which was too much for me, and I had to give him James's tie and made a mess of that. His neck was—but you saw it, no doubt. Then I became James, and my clothes went into his suitcase. I put the letter to the house agents which I found into a parcel with the keys and I walked out. I went to Paris as I had intended, but in unexpected comfort. That it was at his expense made the journey doubly pleasant. Once in Paris, James disappeared—they will find him at the bottom of the Seine—

239

and Fanshawe came home, third class this time, shedding the passport overboard as the boat reached Dover.

"As to why he came home—but it would be a pity to leave you without something unsolved, wouldn't it? Besides, time is short. Good-bye."

The letter ended as abruptly as it had begun. Mallett thrust it into his pocket, called Frant to watch by the dead man and went outside to await the arrival of the ambulance. He felt utterly tired and desperately in need of fresh air. As he reached the street door, a voice called him quietly by name. He looked round and saw Harper standing on the pavement, pale and dishevelled.

"What do you want?" he asked.

"Is he—dead, Inspector?" the young man asked in his turn.

"Yes. How did *you* know?"

"I—I guessed it. It was what I thought he would do," Harper muttered.

Mallett looked at him again. It had stopped raining by now, but his hat and clothes were wet, as though he had been standing in the open for some time.

"How long have you been here?" he asked.

"Quite a long time," was the answer. "I was waiting for you. I saw the police car outside and I didn't care to go in."

He spoke in an oddly subdued manner, humbly even, without a trace of his usual conceit.

"How did you know I would be here? What have you to do with this affair?" the inspector persisted.

Harper drew a deep breath before replying.

"I told him you were coming," he said at last.

"What!"

"As soon as you had explained who Colin James was, I saw that Fanshawe's alibi was destroyed. You said almost as much yourself, in so many words. So as soon as I could, I telephoned to him. I hoped he would get away, but—"

"You hoped to defeat justice, eh?"

"Yes." Harper's voice became more and more apologetic. "I'm sorry, Inspector, I quite see that it was very wrong of me, but I had to."

"What do you mean?"

"You see, he was my father's best friend."

"And helped to ruin him, I'm told."

"Exactly. Although my father always insisted that he was not really to blame. I saw him the day he was released from prison. He promised to help me if he could. Then the morning after the inquest on Ballantine I got this."

He drew from his pocket a crumpled letter which he handed to the inspector. It was in Fanshawe's writing, addressed from Daylesford Court Mansions, and ran as follows:

My dear boy,

Circumstances over which I had no control have prevented me from making any repayment of the debt which I owed to your father. Will you please accept the enclosed by way of some recompense? You will oblige me by not acknowledging this letter, or mentioning to anyone the fact that you have received it. God bless you.

J.F.

"With the letter were banknotes to the value of two thousand pounds," Harper explained. "I didn't know— I swear I didn't know—where the money came from. I mean, I never connected him with Ballantine's death in any way, not until this afternoon in the taxi."

"No?" Mallett's brows shot up.

"No. I didn't know—how could I? Why, Inspector,

241

you must believe me. You've only just tumbled to it your-self," he protested, with a spark of his old arrogance. "And the money—it meant simply everything in the world to me. I didn't think—I didn't let myself think—that that could have anything to do with the murder." The young man's urgent voice broke, and then he added, almost under his breath: "At first."

"At first. And then?"

"And then—God, it was awful! The not knowing, I mean! And not a soul to share one's doubts with!" He shuddered, and went on in quieter tones: "Well, it's over now. I needn't go on deceiving myself, anyway. And Ballantine's bloody creditors can have the money. I haven't spent a bob of it."

"Just a minute," said Mallett. "You've been through a bad time, and I'm not at all sure you don't deserve all you've got, but there's no reason why you should make things worse than they are."

"Worse?" Harper laughed mirthlessly. "I like that!"

"I've been looking through Fanshawe's papers," went on the inspector impassively. "He kept them in apple-pie order, as one might expect. I find that he drew a cheque to self for two thousand pounds on the 18th of this month on an account he kept at the Bank of England in the name of Shaw. It rather looks as though that was his present to you. No doubt we shall be able to prove it by the numbers of the notes."

"Of course you will," said Harper impatiently. "But what is the point of that?"

"Only that this passbook shows that the account had not been operated for five years. The money he stole from Ballantine went into a separate account altogether."

"You mean—"

"I mean, young fellow, that the only matter between us now is the telephone call you made an hour or so ago.

I needn't tell you that you have committed a criminal offence."

"No," said Harper soberly, "you needn't. But it's an offence I shall be proud of having committed to my dying day."

The lights of an ambulance appeared round the corner. While they approached, Mallett remained quite still, staring in front of him.

"What are you going to do with me?" asked the voice at his side.

The inspector turned his head abruptly towards him.

"I think I can make my report without mentioning your name," he jerked out. "Good night, young fellow, and—good luck!"

He moved away to give instructions to the stretcher bearers.